Savannah

A Douglas Powell,
Casey Malone Story

By

B. Benedict Braddock

Savannah. A Douglas Powell, Casey Malone story

Please contact the publisher:

Empathy Books

Humanservicesconsultants@gmail.com

Empathy Books

Thanks to Book designer Usama Bajwa for his cover and interior formatting work.

E-mail: usamabajwa040@gmail.com

Book One: The Common life of Casey Malone

Book Two: Cotton and Candlelight

Book Three: Savannah

Follow Author B. Benedict Braddock on Amazon, facebook, or Instagram for updates on future books in this series.

Table of Contents

Week One

Casey and Douglas had relaxed in the swing every night since they'd arrived in Savannah five days earlier, beneath twinkling white lights and surrounded by poinsettias, on the porch of a grand old mansion that had stood proudly since before the civil war. There was a journal in the historical society's museum, written by a Union Colonel who had made use of the porch swing himself when the Union army had taken over the ten bedroom home for use as a field hospital shortly after the city had fallen in 1864. The army had camped just down the way in the cemetery, moving the stones of confederate soldiers and city residents out of their way in order to pitch tents over the graves as an intended disrespect. The Colonel had relaxed there on the porch of the grand old lady, telling of it all in his journal, claiming moral victories and confessing horrific sins.

The house was in a neighborhood of classic homes, on one of Savannah's famous "squares", spectacular old gardens that were the pride of the garden society and main attraction of the historical district. It was decorated in all its Christmas splendor, like a proper southern belle poised to descend the grand stairwell in a beautiful, shimmering gown. The old homes competed to outdo one another, each more impressive and enchanting than the next, with white, horse-drawn carriages passing by slowly every few minutes to truly transport you back in time to a simpler, and far less hectic place. Casey had fallen immediately in love with the place, allowing it to wash over her and ease her mind of the pain, stress, and worry of past holidays of her childhood.

It had been ten days since Douglas and Casey had stood before a family court judge and officially adopted one another, becoming family in the eyes of the law and declaring an allegiance to one another that no one who knew them would ever doubt. Casey's ribs were still sore from the beating she'd taken just outside of Jefferson while helping to investigate the death of young Jeremy Timmons, whose story had inspired action committees, scholarships, and honest discussions throughout the south. They had barely completed their work on his case when the day had come for the adoption ceremony, and shortly after the car was packed and the two of them headed out for their first official family vacation.

Savannah was a town of ghosts and stories, with a rich culture and often troubling history still preserved in the river-front cotton exchange building and in the old plantations that lay just outside of the city proper. The city's historic district was among the largest in the nation, with antebellum architecture, moss covered old oaks and picturesque parks that dated back to as early as the American revolution. It was a town of art and culture, great food and decadent treats, exciting tours and spectacular sunsets. It seemed like they hadn't stopped eating since they had arrived and so they began an evening ritual of after dinner walks before collapsing into the cushy swing.

Thanksgiving had been the best that either of them had ever experienced. Served out behind the majestic old house in the brick paved courtyard with a stunning view of the rear gardens. The original fountain was still in use, lighted, in the evenings, by submerged pastel bulbs that produced an almost magical effect. The patio tables were all wrought iron, painted in a bright white and finished with comfortable flower patterned cushions. Dinner had been served by candlelight, beneath the prettiest southern sky that anyone could possibly ask for. The Riley's were the perfect hosts, sharing their love for the old city and its history over dinner and one of the best pumpkin pies they had ever tasted.

They had spent the last few days exploring the sights and browsing in the never-ending shops that ran along the riverfront and dotted the entire historic district. They spent hours walking the beaches of Tybee island and feasting on the best seafood the southeast had to offer. They had planned to move on from here and spend a few days in Charleston, perhaps even head up further along the coast and spend some time exploring the beach communities. But Sammy's invitation to take the lead on a human trafficking investgation had been too important to pass up, and at the end of the day this was who they were and what they felt they needed to be spending their time on. Vacation had been nothing short of awesome, but tomorrow it would be back to work.

Casey swung her legs slightly to rock the swing and it seemed to keep time with the soft breeze. It was a gorgeous evening, as they had all been, maybe sixty degrees with clear skies and a cozy view of the line of porch lights extending down the block. Douglas came out through the screen door with a couple cups of coffee, handing her one as he lowered himself down beside her on the swing. "I talked to McAfee. He'll meet up with us for breakfast tomorrow before we head out for the interview."

Casey nodded. "How is it possible to gain ten pounds in five days?"

Douglas smirked into his coffee cup. "I don't think it's quite that bad."

"At least five."

"Well, vacation ends tonight and we should probably get ourselves back on more of a real-life diet again."

"I think it all went to my ass. I can't even button my jeans."

He laughed out loud. "I think you're exaggerating just a little."

"Close though."

"You sure you're okay with cutting vacation a bit short?"

"This sounds like a really important story. We can always take another vacation whenever."

"True enough."

"And this one has been awesome even if it was short."

He reached over and took her hand. "Yes it has."

Sammy had emailed some very basic details to Douglas just that afternoon. They were to meet up with Loren A'mico, a freelance journalist who covered Savannah and often contributed features to the Atlanta Daily. A'mico had apparently stumbled onto something bigger than she was able to handle alone, and she had requested backup from the Daily in order to give the story the time and emphasis it deserved. All she'd said was that it involved human trafficking, and that she had proof that some very heavy players were involved. Douglas had arranged for retired Atlanta Detective Lloyd McAfee to once again be contracted as their lead investigator. Casey, who had earned her stripes on the Timmons case, had been awarded with the title of Investigative journalist. Douglas couldn't tell who was prouder, Casey or himself.

They waved to a couple strolling down the sidewalk and quietly sipped their coffee. "I think this is one of those things I'll never understand," Casey finally spoke.

"What's that?"

"Human trafficking. It's gotta be the most horrible thing in the world. Not much worse than that out there."

"Yeah," Douglas nodded as he looked out over the square. "Were you able to get our stats together?"

"Yes. The government kinda bunches all trafficking statistics in together, whether it's sexual slavery, forced labor, or debt bondage. But all combined, there are an average of a thousand open cases at any one time in the country. They estimate two hundred thousand victims each year in the States alone."

"Gosh," Douglas shook his head. "It's sickening."

"Well, the demand is high. The border states of course have the most initial cases but then New York, L.A., Vegas, and of course here in Atlanta."

"Are the numbers very high here at home?"

"Georgia is number four in the nation. The numbers are really high in Florida and up here both for forced labor and sex trafficking."

"They sell these poor women online like used tools."

"Yup. In every major city and lots of small towns. They say the Super Bowl is the largest market event in the world for sex trafficking. Ten thousand victims in just that one week."

Douglas frowned. "Ages?"

"The average victim is fifteen years old. They start as young as twelve."

Douglas made a few notes in his phone for his interview the next day. "So where are these girls all coming from?"

"All socio-economic backgrounds and education levels from elementary school dropouts to college graduates. Lots of them are teen runaways who were also being sexually abused at home, some straight up kidnapping victims. Lots of girls are just grabbed from some of the poorer communities south of the border and brought into the states through unsecured border areas."

"Thank God for the new wall."

"Yes. But they walk straight through the legal checkpoints as well and claim them as their own kids. Half of the time they're not."

"What do we know about their treatment once they've begun to prostitute them?"

"The government says that seventy percent of all trafficking victims need emergency room care at least once a year due to the excessive physical abuse."

They stayed quiet for a few more moments thinking about the savagery that people so easily inflicted upon one another. Few people suffered more than sex trafficking victims, whose lives meant absolutley nothing to those who profited from their pain. Whatever your sick compulsion might be, your requests would be met. For a price. If that meant that you wanted to kill the poor girl that was delivered to you, go ahead. Your mess would be cleaned up for you and nobody would ever know because nobody would miss the victim. As long as you had enough cash everything was on the table.

Douglas nodded to Casey. "Okay, so tomorrow we'll see what we've got."

"I hope we can put somebody away."

"This is dangerous territory, kid. We need to keep things tight on this and watch our backs. The kinds of people who are involved in this have absolutely no respect for human life."

"I have no respect for theirs either," she answered, "I hope McAfee gets to shoot one of them in the damn face."

Douglas took a sip of his coffee. "We can hope."

They went back to slowly rocking on the swing, but somehow it didn't feel quite the same as it had the past week. Vacation was officially over.

With the morning came the dread of reality. They packed their bags and prepared to leave behind the hundred dollar pillows, gourmet breakfasts, manicured gardens, and, of course, the porch swing that they'd both fallen in love with. The Atlanta Daily would be footing the bill from here on out and there was no way in hell Sammy would keep paying for a luxury bed and breakfast. Nope, they were headed for the Deep South Motel, a fairly nice, fairly clean place in the newer side of town that offered vending machine danish and free instant coffee between six and nine each morning. Douglas and Casey had passed by the day before to take a look and they booked three rooms for themselves and McAfee who was on his way from Atlanta and meeting them at the Motel shortly. Casey met Douglas in the hallway and he grabbed her bag to carry it down the stairs for her. Casey was only one hundred and twenty pounds and he figured her bag might weigh nearly as much.

Once their gear had all been wrestled into the trunk of the Mercedes, they bid the Rileys a fond farewell and headed out. After a few quiet moments of after vacation blues Casey finally broke the silence.

"We should put a swing out on the terrace at home."

Douglas smiled. "You know what? That's a very good idea...let's do it."

"Yeah?"

"Yeah."

"Cool, right?"

"Very cool."

She smiled and turned to look out at the gorgeous wreaths and Christmas displays that adorned the stately old homes. "Three weeks till Christmas."

"Yup, I'm excited. And you and I will be back home for that no matter what."

"We gonna cook?"

"And bake, of course. You think we're fat now?"

Casey laughed. "Maybe we should invite a few people over for Christmas eve and then have Christmas day for just us?"

Douglas nodded. "I think that would be awesome." He glanced over quickly at her.

"I haven't heard you mention Jerry at all. You been talking to him?"

Casey shrugged. "Just a text here and there. To be honest I'm not really feeling it."

They pulled into the motel parking lot and saw that McAfee was already there. He was leaning against his car sipping out of a 7-eleven cup and shooting dart-like stares at anyone who walked within his acceptable boundaries. He managed a weak grin as they pulled in beside him. Casey nodded out her open window. "Old man."

"Malone," he grunted back.

"You're looking good," she said as she climbed out. "I'm lying of course."

McAfee laughed. "Let's see how you look at my age."

"You'll be dead by then so you'll never know."

He grinned again. "True enough."

She gave him a hug and went to sign them all in. Douglas came around and leaned against the car next to him. "How was the ride?"

"I need to get one of those massage things for the car."

"Oh yeah, the heated one?"

"That's right you can get heated ones. Yeah, I'm gonna find me one. So how was your vacation?"

"Too short but awesome. I think it was really good for us to just spend some time alone for a little bit." Douglas smiled. "I'll tell you something Lloyd, I can't even remember her not being in my life. My focus has completely changed."

McAfee put his hand on Douglas' shoulder. "You're good for each other. Everybody can see that. I'm glad for you brother."

Douglas smiled. "Thanks Lloyd."

Casey came out with three room keys and the men reached out their hands.

"Good," McAfee said. "I gotta piss like crazy."

"Well y'all are gonna wait till I check all three rooms and decide which one I like best for myself."

"C'mon Malone, jus' hand one over."

"You heard me."

"Sona of a…"

"Relax old man. Two minutes, tops."

"She's actually serious," he looked at Douglas.

"Yup, she is."

Once Casey had chosen her favorite room, the one she scrunched her nose up at the least, they carried in their bags before walking next door to a dive diner that looked like it had seen much better days.

"Feels like home," McAfee said as they slid into a booth.

"Yeah," Douglas agreed. "I was just thinking the same thing. A good ol' greasy spoon."

"I hope they have the patty sausages," Casey said. "I like them better than the links."

"It's all the same," McAfee grunted.

"It is not. That's like sayin' grits are grits when everybody knows grits are not grits."

McAfee had to agree. "Well, that's true enough."

"Hushpuppies neither."

"When you're right, you're right."

"None of it's gonna be what we've been spoiled with the last week," Douglas said from behind his open menu.

Casey frowned. "Don't we have a meal budget?"

"Yup, greasy spoon breakfast and a couple hot dogs off the cart," McAfee answered.

As it turned out, they all ended up enjoying the southern cooking and pledged that they'd be back each morning of their stay. Douglas brought Lloyd up to date with the small bit of information they'd received from Sammy, explaining who Loren A'mico was and her relationship with the Daily.

"So, we basically don't know anything yet?"

"Nope," Douglas answered. "But I suspect that'll change about a half hour from now. You both ready?"

Casey and Lloyd nodded and the three of them slid back out of the booth.

"Whose car we taking?" Lloyd asked.

"I'll drive," Douglas replied. "You must be wiped out from the ride over."

Loren rented a one room office in a small building not far from the motel. It was a typical meet and run kind of a place, just a spot for quick interviews and to store some files. It was maybe twelve by twelve with a shared restroom in the hallway and not very much natural light. There was a small desk, a loveseat and matching easy chairs, and a striking painting that Douglas thought might be a scene from Forsyth park. Loren herself was neat and professional looking, perhaps thirty-five, slender and maybe even on the athletic side. She wore her dark hair in a tight pony- tail, and her charcoal suit betrayed the fact that she had money that certainly hadn't come from the writing game. They shook hands all around before settling in.

Douglas smiled. "I'm glad we finally have a chance to meet. I've been an admirer of your work for a while now."

Loren beamed at the compliment. "That's a huge compliment coming from you, Douglas. You're a legend."

"Well, I don't know about that but I do appreciate a good story."

"That's why I really wanted to work with you on this. You have a reputation for digging in when things turn harsh and I'm afraid that's a certainty in this case."

"Sammy didn't tell us very much."

"I was contacted a couple months back by a woman named Carly Trainor who works as a waitress at a truck stop out on ninety-five. She took notice of a young girl who began popping up most nights just hanging around the building and running in and out to use the restroom. It didn't take long for her to realize the kid was a prostitute which in itself wasn't that unusual but she was concerned about how young the girl looked. She didn't get involved at first until one night the girl came in with horrible bruising all over her face and a swollen lip."

"Did Carly approach her?" McAfee asked.

"Yes. The first night just to say a quick hello. The second she asked how she was doing. She said the girl just answered with a quick 'fine' and moved along."

"How many women work that plaza?"

"Carly says she sees them come and go. Sometimes ten at a time...sometimes just one or two."

"How old was Carly guessing the kid was?"

"She thought maybe fourteen."

Casey made some notes in her book as McAfee asked his questions. She looked up to ask one of her own. "Did the girl ever say any more than that?"

"Yes," Loren nodded. "About a week in, Carly ran into her in the restroom and the kid was trying to cover up some bruises with makeup. Carly just smiled and said Hi and the girl smiled back a little. Carly told the girl her name and the girl answered with her own...Dede."

"Any further conversation?" Douglas asked.

"Not at first. But over the next couple of weeks they spoke more and more. Dede told Carly some stuff that horrified her. She was afraid that if she called the cops that they'd just treat the kid like any other prostitute and so she decided to contact me instead."

"Did Dede offer up her age?" McAfee asked.

"Yes, she had just turned sixteen."

"She say where she was from?"

"No. Carly thought she seemed afraid to give that up."

"A runaway."

"Yeah, that's my guess."

"Did she give up any details on the people that were abusing her?"

"She gave a lot more than that."

McAfee stood up to pace the room a little. Longer car rides wreaked havoc on his sciatica. He kept his gaze on Loren as he moved. "So, let's just jump into the deep end and then we can back track, okay?"

"Shoot," Loren agreed.

"Did the kid name any names?"

"Oh yes. That's the thing. The reason I called you."

McAfee stopped and nodded. "Give it to us."

"Conrad Nash."

Douglas sat up straight. "The Conrad Nash?"

"Yes."

"State Representative Conrad Nash?"

"One in the same."

"The fuck you say," McAfee grunted.

"That's what I said at first. But I'm into this now you guys, and I'm telling you it's gospel."

"Who's Conrad Nash?" Casey asked.

"A guy who could very well be our next Governor when Teresa Jacobs' term is up."

"A guy that we sure as hell don't wanna play with without rock solid evidence," McAfee added. "This guy is the law and order guy. He's got the endorsement of every police union in the State before he's even announced his candidacy."

"I'm telling you I've got this guy with clean evidence. I've seen some shit with my own eyes. That's why I needed you. If I keep pushing I know I'll be in for a world of hurt."

"What exactly did you see?" Douglas pressed. "Exactly."

"I saw some coyotes deliver a van full of young Mexican girls to a local pimp and none other than Nash himself. They herded them all out of the van and that pervert personally inspected each of them."

McAfee stared at Loren for a moment before starting to pace again. "Goddamnit!"

There was silence in the room for several minutes as the group absorbed the possibly career-ending information.

"So," Casey snapped them out of it, "We should talk to the girls at the truck stop directly."

"Afraid not," Loren shook her head. "The Irish mob are the king shits in Savannah. They didn't want the pimps bringing any heat out there on the highway because their own guys are supplying all the drivers with thousands of dollars worth of pills a day. So they ran them off about three weeks ago and that was that."

"Damn," Douglas closed his notebook. "I would have liked to talk to Dede myself."

"Oh you can do that," Loren replied. "Carly's got her stashed in her apartment."

Loren made the arrangements for Douglas, Casey and McAfee to meet up with Dede the next morning at Carly's apartment. Carly had said that she needed to be up early for her breakfast shift out at the truck stop but that Dede had no worries about meeting with them on her own. They had agreed to meet up with her at ten and were presently back at the diner having yet another horrendously bad for them breakfast.

"I can't even imagine the hell that this girl has gone through," Douglas was saying. "Being handed over from one scumbag to the next day after day."

"You think she's on drugs?" Casey asked.

"Most likely," McAfee answered. "That's how they maintain their control."

"So you think she just ran away and got trapped with these guys?"

"Happens every day."

Casey buttered her short stack before smothering it with some Vermont maple syrup. She caught Douglas smiling a little out of the corner of her eye. "I know. I'm fat as hell."

"No you're not."

"Yes I am and now I can't stop eating. It's like a southern comfort food addiction."

"You're a buck thirty at the most," McAfee smirked.

"Yup and usually a buck twenty."

"So order the fruit plate," he laughed.

"Yeah, okay. I think not."

The men laughed and Douglas checked his watch. "Eat up. We're outta here in fifteen."

The ride wasn't far and it was hardly the disaster Atlanta traffic that they were used to. Carly lived in a second floor apartment right on the line between the old city and new. Her building though was definitely part of the old, with beautiful architecture and ornate railings across the front of the upper level terraces. The tree lined street felt dense and perpetually cloaked in their shade, making the cool morning feel slightly cooler. Savannah and its historic neighborhoods had a way of making you feel like pouring a big cup of coffee and settling in with a good book.

They found the stairwell along the side of the building and made their way up. Number seven was the second door down and McAfee gave it a couple taps.

When the door opened a few seconds later it was clear why Carly had been so concerned about this young girl. She was tiny for sure and looked like she could pass for thirteen.She had dark hair and eyes and wore a t-shirt that looked two sizes too big for her and was probably loaned to her by Carly. She looked at them with what could only be described as disinterest and waited for one of them to speak first. Douglas found himself transported right back to the North Georgia women's reception center that very first day he met Casey. Dede had that same lost look and expression of surrender. He smiled and offered his hand. "Hi Dede, I'm Douglas and this is Lloyd and Casey. She looked from face to face, settling for a moment on Casey before shrugging and stepping aside for them to enter. "Come in."

The apartment was fairly large for a one bedroom as was usual for these older units. It was decorated warmly but clearly on the cheap but was clean and obviously cared for. Dede gestured for them to sit and the three of them settled in beside each other on the oversize sofa.

"Y'all want any sweet tea or somethin?" she asked.

First question answered, Douglas thought. At least in part. This kid was a southern girl, maybe even from Georgia but she was Dixie for sure. They all thanked her but said they were fine and she shrugged and plopped down into a large chair opposite them. Douglas smiled inwardly as Casey began the conversation. "You a peach, girl? You sound like you was raised 'bout where I'm from near Concord," she smiled.

Dede smiled just slightly in kind. "Mississippi."

"Oh, okay. I have a friend that grew up right around Gulfport. You from 'round there?"

"So you wanted to ask me some questions about the truck stop?" she asked.

There it was, Douglas thought, that all familiar evasion. It was very much like talking with a younger Casey Malone.

"If you don't mind Dede," he began. "We'd like to see if there's some way we can help prevent what happened to you from happening to other girls."

"What y'all wanna know?"

"Well, for starters, how did you end up with these men to begin with?"

Dede seemed to get lost in her own thoughts for a few long moments. Casey went to say something but McAfee placed his hand on hers and she understood that he wanted her to wait. After a short bit she looked back up at them. "It's a long story. I'm not really sure where to start."

"Wherever you think you should, sweetie. We're in no hurry at all," Douglas answered. She nodded and slowly began to tell her story.

Bell Mississippi was on the southwest border of the state within a stone's throw of Louisiana. It was deep-south and impoverished, forgotten in comparison to New Orleans and the coastal beach areas that were not very far off. The unemployment rate in the County stayed up near forty percent and it didn't matter even a little bit what political party was in office or what promises they might have made to get there. The houses were run down and the streets were in disrepair. The schools were forever lacking in supplies and proper staffing levels and they struggled to even hold onto their "D" rating. There were only two cops in the town, the first being a falling down drunk and the second just couldn't give a shit. It all brewed up into a recipe for disaster if you were a fourteen year old girl just trying to have any semblance of a life.

As far as families went in Bell, Dede was fortunate to even have one. Most of her friends were being raised by single Moms who counted on food stamps and section eight for their survival. Her Daddy didn't have much of a job but at least he had one, mucking out stalls, burning trash, feeding animals and doing light repairs for a small farm just outside of town. It didn't pay all that much but they were slightly better off than most of the folks they knew. On the weekends he would do some car repair work out on the front lawn and people would pay him twenty bucks or so to put in an alternator or replace a sensor. Most important was he treated Dede and her Mama with nothing but pure love, working day after day to take care of them even when his back was screaming and his hands all torn up.

Dede was a good student and actually enjoyed her classes and homework. Mostly she enjoyed making her Mama and Daddy proud when she'd bring home a good report card with nice comments from her teacher. She liked to help her Mama out with housework as well, mostly cooking because she loved learning new recipes and how to search through the mail fliers for the right coupons that helped to save Daddy some money. Neither Mama or Daddy could read very well, so after dinner each evening Dede would read a bit to them from the books she checked out of the school library and it made her feel good to see the pure pride on their faces as she read. They'd just sit there hand in hand and exchange silent looks as she went on, before telling her it was time to get on with her homework and lay out her clothes for the next day. They were poor, she knew it, but they were happy and loved each other and things in their house were just fine. Right up until the day her Daddy died.

With poverty comes sacrifice. You have to decide what to spend your money on and what things are just not that important. For Dede's Dad, her school clothes and supplies and making sure that Mama had all the money she needed for groceries came first. Getting to the Doctor to find out why he kept having chest pain was just not on the top of the list. He dropped dead at work, out in the back forty on his way to gather a wagon load of wood to cut and split for the colder months coming up. By the time his boss man found him he'd already been gone for a few hours, slumped over the wheel of the tractor like he was gonna drive the rusty old thing right on into the next life. And with his death their happy home life died too. The money dried up in a week, the electric was off in two, and within a month it was feelin' like they might starve to death.

Her Mama loved her. There was never any doubt. The woman would have given her the world if she'd had it to give. But when you have nuthin and no way of ever gettin' nuthin you have to start to look to others for help. For a poor woman in a dirt road town in a county with a forty percent unemployment rate there was only one way to get any help at all, and only one way to pay for it. "I'm still young enough to get a man to take a shine", she'd say to Dede. "It damn sure ain't gonna be like it was with your Daddy but we need to think about getting you through school and the hell outta here."

It was only nine weeks since Daddy passed on when Dennis moved in. He drove a dump truck for the county which was a real good job for a man to have and he even got a holiday bonus just before Christmas each year. Problem was he was married and already had two kids to support. He was only gonna spend a night or two a week with her Mama and the rest back home with his wife. When her Mama had asked won't his wife get mad he just smirked and said , "She ain't gonna say shit." It was all just fine as far as her Mama was concerned. Two days a week she'd do whatever nasty thing it was that fat ugly Dennis wanted her to do and the rest of the week it was just the two of them with plenty of food to eat and the lights still on. Dede didn't like it, she flat out hated it in fact, but she was fourteen which meant she had no way of doing anything about it.

A few months went by like that, Mama wasn't crying as much at night as she had been right after her Daddy died and Dennis even gave them a little extra spending money to get some new clothes from the discount store. Dede missed her Dad terribly but even she began to see a pathway through to a better future for her and Mama both. She dreamed about being able to go away to college at Mississippi State and hoped to someday work in business and be able to buy her Mama a big house and lots of pretty clothes. From time to time she'd even think about maybe one day moving to New York or Miami or any of those places where people became rich and had everything they wanted. But for now it was just dusty old Bell, and listening to disgusting Dennis chew with his mouth open like a goat.

School was fine. She had lots of friends and pretty much everybody was in the same boat. All her classmates hugged her when her Daddy passed and a couple of their Moms even stopped by with casseroles or fresh baked bread for her and Mama. Her grades stayed good because she wanted more than ever for her Mama to be proud of her and smile the way she always did on report card day. She had even begun thinking of maybe trying out for the school play or maybe even learning to play an instrument. It was only freshman year, she had three more to go after that, but if things stayed as they were it wouldn't be all that bad. But they didn't.

The first time was when her Mama got an interview to do cleaning for the nursing home. Jobs were hard to find and hundreds of women had applied. So when Mama had gotten the call she was so excited she looked like she might burst. It was a Saturday, about three in the afternoon when she left for her three-thirty appointment. She headed out in Daddy's beat up old truck that sounded like it might not even get her there. Dede waved from the front yard and watched her drive all the way to the end of their street. She found herself smiling at the thought of more money coming into the house. It sure would be nice not to have to rely on Dennis for every penny.

He was stretched out in her Daddy's recliner watching his game when she walked back into the house. A big bowl of chips rested in his lap as he sipped cheap beer and yelled at the screen. He turned to look at her quickly before turning right back to the screen. "Shut that door girl. Bills are high enough without heatin' the damn porch."

She did as she was told before heading back to her room to work on her book report. It was hard to concentrate with him out there either hooting or hollerin' at the t.v. He finally quieted down after about ten minutes and she was able to start her work in peace.

She was laying on her bed writing in her notebook when her bedroom door opened. She was surprised because he had never come into her room before. "Half-time", he smiled.

"Umm, you need to knock."

"I don't need to do jack shit in my own damn house girl."

She went back to her writing. "It's my Mama's house. And my Daddy's."

"Well, your dead daddy ain't here and your Mama don't put the food on the table."

She ignored him and kept writing.

"You know," he said more quietly as he leaned against the door frame, "you ain't been nuthin' but disrespectful to me since I got here. You should show a little goddamn gratitude for what I do for you."

She looked up again. "I have not been disrespectful. I always do what you tell me to."

"With a roll of your damn eyes."

"That's not true. I never..."

"Hell yes you do. All's I gotta do is walk in and you make a face. You wouldn't even have a light to do your homework if I didn't pay for it."

"Well, I am grateful and I'm sorry if I ever rolled my eyes at you."

Dennis pulled out her old desk chair, a metal folding one that her Daddy had bought for her at a yard sale, and took a seat. Dede sat up to look at him so that he wouldn't say she was disrespectful for not paying attention.

"I work very hard for my money," he went on. "And I can have any woman I want in this County and your Mama damn well knows it. It ain't easy for a woman with a kid to feed to get hold of a guy like me."

"My Mama is very pretty."

"She ain't bad,"

"And smart and sweet."

"She can cook pretty good."

"Lots of guys would like dating her."

"Dating," he smirked. "Right."

Dennis heard the game announcer come back on and stood up. "Well, nice talking to you."

"You too," she lied.

He turned a bit as if to leave and she laid back down to finish her work. He stopped and pushed the chair back in under the desk. Then he slapped her bottom. At first she was a little stunned, unsure of how to take it. Was he just being playful with this kid that he was in this step-dad role with? Or was it something...else. He continued out the door without another word or glance in her direction and she was left to wonder... and hope not.

Casey's stomach had tightened up as soon as Dede mentioned Dennis entering her room. She knew this story all too well and had lived that pain for nearly her entire childhood. She took a deep breath as Dede fell off into her own thoughts and turned to look at Douglas who was already looking back at her worriedly. She gave him a sad smile and he responded in kind, the wordless exchange of two people who had become so close that they didn't need to speak to one another to communicate. After a few moments of quiet McAfee nodded to Douglas.

"Well," Douglas smiled at Dede. "How about we continue our talk tomorrow? Maybe we can take you to lunch if you're up to it?"

Dede nodded. "Okay. But Carly said I should stay out of sight."

"Nobody's gonna mess with you when you're with us," McAfee answered. "And we'll be very careful to make sure nobody follows us back home after lunch."

"Okay. I'll be ready."

Casey was stretched out on her motel bed, surrounded by file folders that Loren had supplied with all the information she'd gathered so far. Douglas and McAfee sat on the sofa reading through another stack.

"Loren's been thorough," Douglas said

"Yeah," McAfee agreed. "She's on the ball."

"I don't think she wants to be in on it much further. She seems really spooked."

"Yeah, well, Conrad Nash is a big shit all 'round Georgia but especially here in his own district. Plus I'm sure actually seeing him with the victims must have been scary for her."

"I'm more than a little concerned myself here Lloyd. I'm used to dealing with corrupt politicians but this..."

"I know. We need to try to get a handle on what we're up against. I'll try to ask Dede some real direct questions to try and figure out just who's involved. I mean, at this point it could be anything from small town scumbags to the cartels."

"My gut's already screaming that Nash isn't in business with nobody's. This could get bad really fast."

"You guys see the lake at night yet?" Casey asked.

"No", they answered in unison.

The lake was neither large nor small, perhaps about 300 acres. It stretched out behind the motel and was popular with both hobby fishermen and jet skiers alike. Each room had a back door which opened up to a "patio". Painted but peeling concrete slabs that were slowly losing a battle to the grass that was reclaiming the space inch by inch along its edges. The patios fit in well with the half maintained and fairly clean theme the motel had going. The three of them stood looking out over the now darkened waters, enjoying the peacefulness as the moonlight caused an almost shimmering effect. All around the lake Christmas lights twinkled from docks and the roofline of homes. Straight across the lake someone had a fire burning in a pit and they could smell the hickory from where they stood. Casey stood between the two men and looped her arms into theirs.

"The calm before the storm."

"It's beautiful," Douglas answered. "Gets you in the Christmas spirit."

"We should order a pizza," she said softly.

The two men laughed.

"I swear I don't know where you put it," McAfee grinned.

"So...you guys hungry?

The morning brought a misty rain, embracing Casey in the melancholy feeling that often came with knowing an uncomfortable conversation was about to take place. She sat alone in her room looking out the front window at the Motel light as it flickered off for the day. It was only seven and she was surprised that she had woken so early on a day that she could have slept in just a little. There was something about Dede's story that had touched her and brought her back to her own struggles with poverty and loneliness. She was certain that the story was about to turn much darker, and she felt for this kid who had clearly suffered some unimaginable horrors. She thought back to when she was fourteen, the worst of times. Some men could be disgusting. Their own harmful desires and twisted obsessions leading them to do irreparable harm to young people who would never recover from the trauma. She was one of them. If she could get through one single week without one of her nightmares she'd be thrilled. Just one night that she didn't jump out of her own skin soaked in sweat and with her blood pumping so hard she could feel it behind her eyes. She'd given up on therapy, knowing that this was a life sentence for her.

She stood up to lay out her clothes for the day, choosing a pair of jeans and a cute top she'd bought at the outlets just outside of Atlanta on a shopping day with Emma and Sasha. Her part time job at the Atlanta Daily had provided some awesome spending money especially since Douglas refused to let her chip in one single dime toward the household expenses. He said he wanted her to just focus on her college courses and on being a normal carefree young woman for a while. Except, of course, when she was helping to catch criminals, murderers and apparently now human traffickers. But she loved it, and he knew that. This was her new therapy, recognizing the pain in others and fighting like hell to do something about it. The fact that she could do it side by side with her new Dad made it just that much more awesome.

Casey showered and changed, obsessing for a few minutes in front of the mirror on whether to put her hair up or leave it down. She decided on down, like she did most days, but liked having the option just the same. She thought about texting Jerry to see how he was doing but wasn't sure it was the right move. After all, wasn't the guy supposed to pursue the girl? But maybe he was just trying to be nice and give her and Douglas a little space to spend time together. Truth be told she just wasn't really feeling it. He was a nice guy, good looking and caring, but...what? She didn't really know. Maybe it was just her. There was no doubt that she was more than a little bit damaged. Who wouldn't be? But he just wasn't doing it for her. It was more of an inconvenience setting aside time to spend with him than it was exciting or even happy. She decided against texting him, checked the time and saw it was eight-thirty, and headed out the door to meet the guys for breakfast at their new spot next door.

The grayness of the day was clearly affecting them all and they ate in relative silence for a while. Casey had slid into the booth near to the window so she could watch the local commuter traffic pass by. She had always loved the rain. It was like a blanket of comfort somehow, the cleansing that the world needed if only for a few hours. It was an unusual rain for Georgia. Typically December was slightly cooler and dry, as near to perfect as you could hope for especially if you loved the outdoors. She and Douglas had even talked about maybe heading up into the mountains and perhaps renting a little cabin for a few days. But that was when they were still in the planning stages of their trip, before Sammy had invited them to take on this new investigation for the Daily. Putting an end to the misery of these young women was far more important than roasting some marshmallows or checking out the vibrant colors of late fall. But they would get there eventually. They had nothing but time.

Douglas downed his last bit of coffee and turned his attention to Casey and McAfee. "You've got the lead today kid," he told her.

She was a little surprised. "Me? Why?"

"You can connect with her. If things look too rough for her to talk about in front of Lloyd and I then we'll excuse ourselves and you help her to get out whatever she needs to."

"We really need to know exactly who we're dealing with," McAfee added. "As many names as possible and descriptions of places. An address is great but if not what was the color of the place? The colors of the door or shutters? Was it a brick building or modern? Apartments or offices? A house or a boat? How did they transport them? If it was a truck or a bus what color and was there a name on it? Did they take her shopping for clothes or food? If so, when and where?"

"Okay," she nodded. "I got it."

"Alright," Douglas patted her hand. "Let's head back next door to jot down some interview questions as a guide. We'll head over to Dede at eleven-thirty.

They knocked on Carly's apartment door at noon on the nose and Dede opened it immediately. She was dressed in jeans and another slightly oversized t-shirt and Douglas thought about trying to get her a little bit of a clothing allowance from the Daily. After all, they paid for information all the time and this could prove to be one of their biggest stories since, well, Casey Malone's. The paper should be able to kick in a couple hundred so the kid could get some clothes that fit her. Something to feel like it was her own.

"Y'all want to come in for a minute?" She asked them.

"We can just head out if you're ready," Casey smiled.

"Okay then."

Dede locked the door with the key Carly had loaned her and led the three of them back down the stairs, stopping for a moment to admire Douglas' black Mercedes.

Casey opened the back door and invited Dede to slide in before following her inside. McAfee climbed into the passenger seat as Douglas walked back around to climb behind the wheel.

It was still drizzling, but no place took to rain as well as Savannah. If anything it seemed to bring out its more gothic qualities and the serene beauty of the wrought iron gates, centuries old buildings and historic cemeteries. Vampire stuff, Casey's absolute favorite.

"What kind of food do you like?" She asked Dede.

"Don't matter."

"Anything you want. We can get some seafood, or Mexican, Chinese, or just some burgers and fries."

"You choose."

"Pizza it is," Casey answered.

Douglas smiled into the rearview and began searching for a pizza place.

"I like your sneakers," Dede told her without actually looking at her.

"Oh thanks. I don't usually go for pink, or anything girly actually, but my friends talked me into it."

"They're pretty."

Casey glanced quickly down at Dede's worn out sneakers.

"You and I should shop one day."

Dede looked at her as if trying to decide if she meant it. "Really?"

"Yeah, it'll be fun."

Dede smiled just slightly. "Okay."

"Okay, cool."

Douglas found a corner pizza shop and managed to parallel park only a few spaces down from the front door. Before they could unfasten their seat belts Douglas' phone buzzed and he checked his text messages. "Oh geez, Lloyd. Look at this. I swear they can't get along without us."

He passed his phone to McAfee who grunted. "Of course not."

"Hey girls," Douglas turned around in the front seat to face them. "Y'all go on and get yourselves some food. We have to take care of a little business for the paper and it might take a little bit."

Casey nodded, understanding that the men were trying to leave them alone to talk and that McAfee was in fact the one who had texted Douglas.

"Okay Pops," she answered with her palm outstretched. "Gold card please."

Douglas smirked and handed her two twenties. "Nice try. Feel free to get dessert."

The two girls climbed out of the back. "And a receipt!" Douglas called after them.

The place was small and cozy, with an old world feel and yet recently updated. There was only one other couple in the restaurant and Casey led Dede to the booth that was farthest away and would provide the needed privacy. The young waitress came over immediately and they ordered a large pepperoni and a couple sweet teas.

After she hustled away to put in their order Casey offered her best reassuring smile. "You mind if I write a couple things down as we talk? It's just so I don't forget any of the details you can give me."

Dede shrugged. "It's okay."

"So I guess we should start with...oh damn girl look behind you at the poster. They have homemade cheesecake!"

Dede turned and laughed a little. "Looks good."

"Sorry, I'm easily distracted by food."

Dede turned back to her looking a whole lot less tense. Bingo.

"Anyway," Casey continued. You were telling us about your Mama's new boyfriend. Dennis, right?"

"Yeah."

"Okay. You want to tell me what happened while it's just us girls?"

Dede nodded.

It had been a couple of weeks since Dennis had invaded her space and he seemed to pay Dede even less attention than normal. Her Mama got the part time housekeeping position which was a really big deal so that they'd have a little bit of cash all on their own without needing to ask him for every little thing. It was excruciating for a fourteen year old girl to have to ask some strange older guy for a few bucks to buy tampons but he insisted on knowing what every dime was for. Probably just because he enjoyed her discomfort so much. He continued coming by a couple nights a week and kept up his part of the agreement by paying their cheap rent and utility bills. Her Mama's shift was normally early mornings and she would be gone before Dede woke up for school. She was always independent in that way, getting herself up and dressed, getting her own breakfast and to school on time. She always woke up right when her alarm went off and went about her regular routine. Right up until the day she woke up to see Dennis sitting beside her bed watching her.

She had nearly jumped out of her own skin. Her heart had never beat that fast, not even when she ran laps during gym class and the last one to finish had to do twenty push-ups. She had instinctively pulled her sheet up over her bare legs and stared back at him incredulously. What the heck was this guy doing in her room? Who did he think he was invading her privacy like this. Worse even than last time because she had been sound asleep. How long had he even been here? Had he come in at six when Mama left for work?

"Why are you in here?" she demanded.

"What did I tell you last time? This is my house now. I go wherever the hell I want."

"You need to get out. I have to get ready for school."

"Who's stopping you?"

"I have to get dressed."

"Who's stopping you?"

"Get out." She tried to sound strong but her voice was trembling just like the rest of her. He just smirked.

"Please. I need to get ready for school."

"You need... your Mama needs. What about what I need?"

She didn't know what to say. She didn't understand. Her silence seemed to annoy him even more. He leaned toward her. "Did you hear my question?"

"Yes Sir. I don't…"

"Don't what? I asked you what about what I need?"

Her mind was racing, searching for an answer, considering ways to escape.

"What...what do you need?"

Twenty minutes later she was in the shower, already late but unable to stop scrubbing. Scrubbing until her skin was raw and the pain brought her back to reality. Her tears fell away, mixing with the water from the showerhead and straight down the drain as though they meant nothing at all. She couldn't stop herself from shaking even though it was warm in the room and warmer still beneath the steaming water. She had heard his loud truck muffler as he pulled away, headed off for his day without a concern in the world, leaving her alone in the shower as her own world fell even farther apart. She thought of her Daddy and sobbed harder. Was he looking down on her? Did he see what had happened?

Casey reached across the table to hold Dede's hand just as the waitress arrived at their table with the pizza. She pulled her hand away slowly so that the young woman could put it down between them. It smelled amazing and she thought she saw the tiniest of smiles from Dede.

"Wow, It looks awesome," Casey said.

Dede nodded.

"Can I get you two anything else? Some extra cheese?"

"Oh yeah, always the extra cheese," Casey answered. This time Dede couldn't help but laugh a little.

"I know," Casey grinned. "When it comes to food I'm all in."

"Is pizza your favorite?" Dede asked her.

"Pizza, tacos, cheeseburgers."

"Me too."

They each grabbed a slice and dug in. It tasted as good as it looked.

"You know," Casey covered her mouth as she chewed. "You and I pretty much share the same story."

"We do?"

"Yeah, though in my case it was my own Dad."

Dede looked her straight in the eye. "Oh no. I'm really sorry Casey."

Casey put her slice down and wiped her mouth. "We can do something to stop what happened to you from happening to other girls. You and me."

"He'll just deny it."

"I'm not talkin' about that piece of shit. But we'll get his ass too. I mean the guys who have been hurting you since then. If you can tell me everything you remember then Douglas and Lloyd will handle it."

Dede looked as if she was going to cry. "I'm really scared."

Casey pushed the pizza out of the way and reached over to grab her hands again. "I was too. Until I met Douglas. You can trust them Dede."

The waitress came back. "All done already?"

"Hell no," Casey answered. "We're gonna eat all that and some cheesecake too."

Dede laughed again as the smiling waitress walked back to her counter.

"Okay," Dede nodded.

"Okay," Casey smiled. "I'm gonna let go now and eat this pizza."

Savannah had always had its secrets. Clandestine affairs, covert business, members only groups that would die before they gave up a single fact. There was great wealth in the city and oftentimes with great wealth came corruption and perversion. Money had a way of erasing the sins of those with the privilege to yield it and wield it. Behind the canes and fedoras, sundresses and umbrellas, there sometimes lurked a seediness and sinister underbelly of an old town with long standing ways of doing things. Douglas, McAfee and Casey sat a half block down from

Conrad Nash's seven bedroom historic townhouse and watched as the trappings of old money came and went. Here and there, a Rolls or Bentley would pass by and neighborhood residents strolled leisurely along brick walkways with a nanny pushing a baby carriage along a few yards back.

Nash's house was certainly as impressive as it was imposing. The tall, black iron gates with menacing looking crows welded on top gave the impression of a dark fortress. Perhaps, Casey thought, this guy was a vampire. In a way, she figured, he certainly was.

"How much you think?" McAfee asked.

"Easy four million," Douglas answered.

"From serving as a public rep?"

"From whatever business the Nash family has been into the past few hundred years."

"The Governor's mansion might be a step down."

"Maybe in the trappings, but not in the prestige."

"Maybe that business they've been into so long is buying and selling helpless girls," Casey jumped in.

"We need more information," McAfee answered over his shoulder.

"I'm meeting with her again tomorrow. I didn't wanna push too much today."

"Rapport is important," Douglas answered. "You're doing really well."

They sat and watched in silence for a while longer, not really expecting anything of any significance to happen but more soaking in the atmosphere and looking for some type of inspiration on how to proceed. Tomorrow, hopefully, they would begin to understand how this small town southern girl ended up under the control of human traffickers. It tended to usually be a straightforward story. Runaways were offered shelter, oftentimes by another female so that the intended victim would feel safe. Then came the demand for repayment of that hospitality, drugs to diminish the will to fight, complete reliance on those who held you so that you had no resources at all should you manage to escape. It was a story that they'd all heard many times before, a history that repeated itself over and over. But as long as kids were abused or neglected at home there would continue to be runaways. And as long as there were runaways there would be victims.

Douglas checked his watch. "Well, he's not gonna pop out of his house with a bunch of kidnapped girls. We'll probably need to set up surveillance on him and I guess this will be the best place to start from. Casey, as soon as Dede confirms to you directly that Nash is our man we'll get going."

"Okay. I think maybe she'll get to that tomorrow."

"Don't push her but we're not here investigating whatever it was that took place at home...as horrible as that may be. This is a sex trafficking and criminal corruption story. Start to steer her a bit so we can get the info we need to kick things off. The Daily's not gonna give us too much time to get there."

"I understand," Casey answered. "I just feel bad to push."

"Welcome to investigative journalism. Half the job is feeling that way."

Casey nodded.

"Alright," Douglas started the car. Back to our diner. I'm starved."

They climbed into their favorite booth and Douglas decided to give Sammy a call on speaker and give her an update on the plan. They placed their order first, a hot open turkey sandwich for Douglas, a medium well burger and fries for McAfee, and a couple scoops of ice cream for Casey who was still stuffed with pizza. Sammy picked up on the third ring.

"Yo."

"Hey," Douglas answered. Got you on speaker with Mac and Casey."

"Nice of you to check in finally."

""Not much to report, boss lady. You know I don't like to bother you for nothing."

"Yeah right. Since when?"

Douglas smiled. "You wanna talk to us or not?"

"Y'all sitting somewhere stuffing your faces?"

"About to. We're at the diner near the motel."

"Sounds charming. So what you got for me?"

"So far some hearsay that Conrad Nash is a sex traficker but we're hoping that tomorrow it comes straight from the victim."

"Make sure your shit is tight on this one, Powell. Don't you get me jammed up."

"We're moving carefully," McAfee answered. "And we will have rock solid surveillance before any fingers are pointed."

"You better. And what about you Malone? What have you done for me lately?"

Casey looked up from her phone. "Huh? What'd you say?"

"God's sake."

Douglas smirked.

"What'd she say?" Casey whispered.

"I can hear you whispering Malone. I said what are you doing to earn your salary?"

"What you think I'm doing? I'm handling my shit. I'm interviewing the victim and getting everything we need."

Sammy sighed into the phone.

"The three of you..."

"It's all good," Douglas assured her. "I'll get hold of you tomorrow evening and the story will be much fuller."

"Tick tock Powell. Got it?"

"Got it boss."

Sammy hung up without another word, just in time for the food to arrive at the table.

"Why you gotta piss her off Malone?" McAfee grunted.

Casey shovelled a spoonful of strawberry ice cream into her mouth and looked surprised. "What are you talkin' about? She asked and I answered."

"You have to learn tact," he went on. "And finesse."

She rolled her eyes. "please. She talks the same way. Nobody's crying."

"Yeah but she's the boss."

"Maybe I'll be your boss one day. Maybe you should start kissing my ass now."

"Yeah okay. Dream on."

Douglas cut up his turkey and laughed. "Can you imagine if Casey ended up taking Sammy's place one day?"

"Good lord. Don't even." McAfee shook his head.

"I'm gonna go easy on you Mac," Casey smiled. "All's you gotta do is say yes Miss and no Miss."

"Keep your fantasies to yourself Malone. Now focus, what's the plan for tomorrow?"

"Shopping."

"Say what?"

"I said shopping. I'm taking Dede shopping. I'm gonna need some cash by the way," she looked at Douglas. "Everything will be cool and casual and friendly and she will feel better about opening up to me."

Douglas pursed his lips as he scooped up some mashed potatoes. "That actually sounds like a good idea, kid. Get her the sneakers she needs and an outfit that fits her right. Maybe a girls day out will get us where we need to be. Just talk as you shop."

"About the case," McAfee jumped in. "Not about your books and movies and vampires and boy bands and all that other dumb shit."

Casey frowned. "You really should hope I'm never your boss."

"Hopefully I'll be long dead by then."

Dede climbed into the backseat of the uber beside Casey. They had agreed to meet up at ten in the morning and she had been waiting by the curb when the car pulled up at nine fifty-three. Casey was happy to see that she was smiling and looked like a normal sixteen year old girl should, carefree and ready for a fun day of shopping.

"You ready to do some damage to the Daily's credit card?"

Dede laughed. "You better not do too much damage or they'll fire you."

"Sammy will never fire me. They love me too much around there."

"You sure this is okay? For real?"

"It's all approved and we're good to go."

Casey asked the driver to continue on to the mall and they settled in for the short ride.

"Carly told me about you," Dede said quietly. "About your...case."

"Did she?"

"Yeah."

"And what do you think about all that? You gonna run away screaming?"

Dede smiled. "No. I wish I had been as strong as you. If I wasn't so scared I could've protected myself."

Casey took hold of Dede's hand. "It's different for everybody. Nobody's circumstances are the same. I did what I had to do to survive and so did you."

Dede looked at her hesitantly. "Do you ever...like, wish you hadn't?"

Casey smiled. "I wish I hadn't needed to. There's a difference. But if I hadn't, I wouldn't be here on my way to go shopping right now with you. It sucks, yeah. I have nightmares all the time. But, I dunno, life isn't always up to us. We can't control what other people throw our way, we can only respond to it."

They reached the mall and thanked the completely disinterested driver before heading in through the food court doors. It was a Wednesday morning and the Mall had just opened at ten and so the place was still fairly empty.

"So," Casey looked Dede up and down. "What's your style girl? Sophisticated sexy, tomboy sexy, nerdy sexy?"

Dede laughed. "I don't think I have a style. What do you think?"

"Okay, I say we just walk around some stores and if you see something you like just call out. And we need to hit up the Nike outlet and get you some new kicks for sure."

They walked down beneath the skylights that filled the mall with beautiful rays of morning sun. Casey spotted a store called, 'Young Miss.'

"How about that place? We're both young misses."

Dede smiled. "Okay."

Casey took her by the arm and they made their way inside, stopping by a clearance rack of jeans to see if anything caught their interest.

"So, while we're looking around do you feel like telling me more about what happened after Dennis...you know, after Dennis." She pulled a pair of bleached jeans from the rack. "Do people still wear these?"

"I think they're coming back," Dede nodded.

"Is all of 1985 coming back?" Casey frowned.

Dede laughed out loud as Casey had hoped. She wanted the conversation to stay casual. Dede had suffered through quite enough tension and stress already.

"Let's hope not," Dede answered.

They moved on to the next rack and browsed through some retro rock and roll t-shirts that they both seemed to agree on. Dede began to talk and Casey continued to pull hangers off the rack and check out the shirts. Keep it casual, she thought, and help this kid get her story out.

She had left that very day, Dede said, leaving a note for her Mama that simply said not to worry, that she would be with friends for a while and get in contact real soon. Her Mama had given her a little spending money and she had fortunately saved it all. She wasn't sure how far eighty bucks would get her but she was determined to make sure it was far away from home. There must be places that would hire her to clean or wash dishes or something, she thought. She could get a full time job and go to school at night to get her GED. She was still only fourteen but if she lied about her age and found a job off the books like Mama talked about then it shouldn't be a problem to pull it off. She knew there were places out there that offered more opportunity than this spit across town. But whatever happened, she was leaving. She refused to be in that house as long as Dennis was still around.

Dede hitched about an hour out to Natchez, then stood looking at the board and trying to decide where in the world to go. The lady at the counter said the next bus was leaving for Atlanta in an hour, and since time was of the essence she bought the ticket. It cost her forty-seven bucks for the ticket, leaving her only thirty-three in her pocket. She bought a water and candy bar from the machine and climbed onto the bus, making her way to a window seat about halfway down the aisle. She sat quietly by herself and waited for the bus to roll out, watching her own tearful face reflect back at her from the freshly cleaned window.

She wasn't sure if she had been dreaming the whole time or not as the commotion of departing passengers woke her from a deep sleep. She glanced around in a state of bleariness for a moment to get her bearings.

"I was just gonna wake you baby," an older black lady told her, "we're in Atlanta love."

Dede wiped her eyes. "How long was I out?"

"Oh, you were out when I got on honey, so about eight hours."

The other riders shuffled their way past her and she waited until she was the only one left. She wasn't in any hurry and felt like she was going to have a panic attack.

She stayed in her seat until most of the others had retrieved their bags outside from the underneath storage before making her way out and grabbing her own small duffel.

The lump in her throat felt like it might suffocate her as she made her way into the bus depot. There were more people in the Atlanta depot station than she had ever seen in her life. She found herself completely terrified and fighting back tears. She spotted a police officer across the crowded floor and decided she was going to just tell him everything. She was only a kid and she needed to be back with her Mama. Let Dennis go somewhere else, like jail. She had only taken about ten steps when she felt a soft hand on her shoulder. She turned to see a warm smile from a girl not too much older than herself.

"Boy I recognize that look," the girl said.

"I'm sorry?"

"You just get in?"

"Yes."

"From a small town someplace I bet."

"How'd you..."

"That was me too, girl. About a year ago. I was scared shitless."

"You came here on your own?"

"Yeah, exactly like you and I must've looked exactly like that."

"What did you do?"

"I met a couple girls really quick and we became roomies. Within a couple days everything was cool and the fear was gone."

"I don't know anybody here at all."

"It'll be fine. You have some money, right?"

Dede looked away.

"Hey," the girl said. "Look, it's cool. You're actually in luck. There were four of us but one just moved out. You can come room with us. We split everything four ways."

Dede frowned. "But I really don't have any money."

"Don't worry about it, I'll spot you to get you started. A pretty girl like you will be working quick."

Dede hesitated. "What kind of jobs are there?"

"Just the usual, you know. I'm Bella by the way." She reached out her hand.

"Hey, Dede."

"Cute."

"Thanks."

Dede looked around the station. She didn't feel quite right about any of this.

"Hey look, no pressure. Just wanted to say Hi cause you looked scared. It was real nice meeting you."

Bella started to walk away.

"Hey," Dede called out. "Wait up."

Casey was very aware that Dede had suddenly stopped talking. She pulled a shirt from the rack and held it up under the teenager's chin. "This one's really cute."

Dede seemed to snap out of the trance she was in. She took the hanger from Casey and looked the shirt over. "Yeah," she smiled. "I like this one."

"We can leave it at the counter while we keep shopping."

"Okay."

They made their way deeper into the store and came across several racks of jeans and capris. The two girls began searching through and Casey commented here and there on which she liked or didn't like. After a few minutes Dede sighed and continued. "Anyway..."

Dede followed Bella out of the bus station toward a nearby parking lot.

"So," she asked, "Why are you at the bus station anyway?"

"Oh," Bella smiled, "I just dropped off my friend. She's going home to visit her folks for a couple weeks."

"Oh. Is she one of your roommates?"

"Oh no. Just a girl I know from around. This is me." Bella pointed to an older Toyota sedan and clicked the button to unlock the doors. "You're gonna like the apartment I think. It's just big enough for all of us and the girls are all really chill."

She opened the back door for Dede to put her bag in before the two girls hopped in front for the ride. "It's only fifteen minutes or so. We're close to downtown which is cool."

Dede smiled. "Sounds really nice."

Bella turned to smile back quickly as she pulled out of the parking lot. "You're so pretty. Everybody's gonna love you. Just watch."

The building looked a whole lot nicer than Dede had expected a bunch of young girls to be able to afford. Bella parked the car in a garage below street level before leading her up a slight ramp and into the main lobby. A doorman tipped his hat to the girls from behind the front desk and Bella gave him a wink before pushing the button for the elevator. They rode up to the ninth floor, turning left to head down the beautifully decorated hallway when the door opened. The carpets and woodwork were prettier than anything Dede had seen before and she found herself a bit worried again about being able to pay her part of the expenses. She said so to Bella.

"No need to worry," Bella put her arm around her shoulder. "Imma make sure you make all the cash you need."

The apartment was spacious and decorated in sleek modern furniture and high-end art, offering a gorgeous view of the city street below that seemed like a work of art all on its own. Dede had seen none of this back home. Nobody in her entire town had seen anything like this.

"There's a bar in the corner, always stocked of course," Bella pointed out. "And all the snacks and stuff you could need in the kitchen. Anything you want just add it to the list on the fridge and the boys will pick it up."

"The boys?"

"Yeah, just some friends who help out with that stuff."

"Oh, okay."

"You're gonna love it here," Bella smiled. "You've never seen money like this before, right?"

Dede shook her head. "It's all amazing."

Another girl came down the hallway with an older man. She kissed his cheek and opened the door and the man left silently.

"So, this is Maria," Bella motioned toward the girl.

Dede guessed immediately that Maria was high as a kite. The girl seemed to barely notice that they had even been in the room. She looked Dede up and down and smirked a little. "You get high?"

Dede shook her head no.

"They're gonna love you chica. Eat you right up."

"Don't pay her any mind," Bella replied. "She likes to talk trash when she's been smoking. Come on, I'll show you your room."

It was like a dream. To think that just the day before she'd been in her tiny closet of a bedroom, with a sagging mattress and wood floor that her Mama had patched with duct tape on account of the holes that had worn through in a couple places. Her curtains had worn so thin from washing that they barely kept any light out at all. But this room, this was fit for a celebrity or something. First of all it was huge, easily twice the size of the master bedroom back in her house. There was a king size bed that felt like heaven when she sat on it to test it out. The sheets and comforter were silk and felt so luxurious she thought it might make her cry. There was a white sofa, a large screen t.v., a small bar and mini-fridge, and the private bathroom with oversize tub and marble finishes that she was sure must have cost a fortune. It made her happy and nervous at the same time. "Bella are you sure…"

"No worries at all," Bella cut her off. I promise you'll be making all the money you need really soon. I'm sure you'll be raking it in by next week. Just relax for now and settle in. Tomorrow we can go shopping and pick out some nice clothes to get you started. Don't worry, you can pay me back whenever."

Casey pulled a pair of black jeans from the rack and showed them to Dede. "These would look really cute on you."

Dede looked suddenly nervous. The memories of falling for the trap in Atlanta were all coming back to her.

"Hey," Casey smiled. "I'm a journalist. We work for the paper, not some lowlife. You can trust me."

Dede nodded. "I know."

She didn't know. That much was obvious. She'd been repeatedly lied to, manipulated and used. Trust me was easy to say but earning it would not come so quickly.

"Maybe with just a nice tee or something," Casey continued. "Then if we get some white sneakers maybe? Why don't you try them on and see what you think."

Dede smiled just slightly and took the jeans from her. Casey sent a quick text to Douglas. This might take a little while.

The food court was just starting to see lunch patrons as they carried their trays to a relatively private table. Dede had chosen a gyro and Casey went for a couple soft tacos. The Mall seemed to still do a fairly vibrant business, considering Malls were dying at an alarming rate all over the country. Alarming especially to Casey who loved nothing more than to stroll through the Malls back home in Atlanta with her friends Emma and Sasha. She just loved the flow of walking from store to store without the worry of searching out a parking space or shoving coins into a meter and then obsessing over the time. This Mall had a huge parking lot that ran all around the enormous structure but in the city there were floors and floors of garage spaces which were awesome for a rainy day shopping excursion.

They ate in silence for a moment, both impressed with the quality of the Mall food.

"So they have a Nike outlet but also New Balance and Skechers," Casey announced as she looked over the paper map she'd grabbed from the information desk.

"I like all of them," Dede answered.

"Me too. I love my sneakers, girl."

"You sure the jeans look good?"

"Smoking."

Dede smiled. "Thanks for this."

"It's fun for me too," Casey answered with her fist over her full mouth. "I wanna try to look for something nice for Douglas for Christmas while we're here too."

"He seems really nice."

Casey wiped her mouth with her napkin. "He saved my life."

"You've been through a lot," Dede nearly whispered.

Casey smiled. "We both have. That's why we deserve a girl's day out."

Dede took a couple more bites before continuing with her story. "I was in the apartment for about a week or so, going out a lot with Bella clothes shopping and to some restaurants. I'd never been to any kind of a restaurant before. I couldn't believe any of it. Atlanta is so beautiful.

All the shining glass and pretty department stores. And the food...it was amazing. Bella said I needed to have some cute outfits to be able to work. Some of the outfits she picked out were just crazy though. You know, skirts that were ridiculously short, too short for me, and stuff that you wouldn't think a store or something would want you wearing if you worked there. She got me some jewelry too, nothing real expensive but not real garbage either. She said I needed to look taken care of. Like I said, I was there about a week before I met Clem."

"Clem?"

"Clement. The fourth bedroom was his."

He had smiled the least sincere smile that Dede had ever seen. Not sarcastic or particularly alarming in any way. Just...fake. Bella had introduced him rather nonchalantly. Oh, this is Clem. He's our fourth. He comes and goes but he's always quiet. This is his place actually, we all sublet."

"Sublet?"

"Yeah, it's a city thing. The lease is in his name but we all rent from him."

"Oh."

"Yeah, it's all good."

"I hope you like it so far." Clem smiled his pretending smile again. "Is your room comfortable enough?"

"Oh yes. It's much nicer than my room back home."

This seemed to please him. "That's really great to hear. And Bella's been helping you get ready for work?"

Dede glanced quickly Bella's way. "Oh yes, and I'll be able to start paying my own way very soon."

"I'm certain you will."

She had been in her room about thirty minutes later when Clem opened her door and came in without knocking. She had nearly jumped out of her skin, still in shock from her experience with Dennis back home. She was angry at her privacy once again being violated and she refused to stand for it.

"We need to talk," he said flatly and sat down on her bed.

"Listen I know it's your place and all but you need to knock."

He stood back up quickly and slapped her. Not particularly violently but firmly enough to get his point across. He shoved her down to sit on her bed and once more took a seat beside her. "I didn't say it was time for you to talk, bitch. You just sit there and listen unless I ask you a question."

Tears came into her eyes. She tried her hardest to fight it and hide her fear but one defied her will and escaped quickly down her cheek. He brushed it away with his thumb and she trembled.

Before Clem had even begun to speak the realization had stung her that she'd made an absolutely dreadful mistake. Whatever was going on here, it wasn't any kind of good, and she found herself wishing that she'd just followed her gut instinct and told that cop in the bus depot that she was a runaway. Clem didn't look angry, or enraged, or even lustful. This wasn't about sex as it had been with Dennis. Clem's face offered no emotion whatsoever. He was matter of fact and even the slap had seemed to her to be all business. Just the way things were.

"I've been supporting you for a week now. Just your share of the rent alone is two grand for that week. Then there's utilities, light and water, cable. Then all the food, a couple pricey restaurants, a grand in new clothes. Lets just call it an even five large. You work for me now. And before you ask, that's not a question or an offer. You're gonna fuckin' do it. Period. The job is easy, all you have to do is entertain some of my closest friends. You'll be real nice to them, cater to them. Do whatever they ask you to do without question."

Dede was in shock. She was young and not at all worldly but she instinctively knew what this was and her heart felt like it might explode right out of her chest it was pumping so hard. "I never agreed to...nobody told me…"

The slap came harder this time, catching most of her left ear and stinging a lot more. It was followed by silence. Clem said nothing and neither did she. He sat motionless, hands between his knees, staring at the floor. Waiting.

"Look! I will not…"

Slap. This one rocked her. Made her dizzy. Then came another, the pain becoming worse with each strike. She was well beyond holding back her tears now and she gasped for breath from the terror of the situation she'd found herself in. He got to his feet in front of her and struck her again, then again. Left cheek, right. She felt her nose begin to run, touched it gingerly...blood. Again he struck.

"Take off your pants," came his calm voice again. She was already nearly unconscious, unable to comply if she wanted to. He shoved her back onto the bed and yanked them off roughly. She stared blurily at the ceiling, missing her Mama.

Casey was heartbroken. The tears rolled freely down her own face and she understood completely why Dede wasn't crying at all. She got up and moved to sit beside her and hugged her tightly. Dede hugged her back, quietly, without emotion, doing as she was trained to do. Casey wouldn't let her go. They stayed that way for a few minutes, passersby probably thinking somebody had broken up with somebody. Some good for nothing boy had run off with the new girl on the block. They wouldn't have been able to imagine. Not looking at the innocent looking face of a sixteen year old going on fourteen. It was brutal and savage, dehumanizing. Not something that goes on in a nice area like this. And that part hadn't, but Casey knew the worst part of the story was still to come.

Weren't men supposed to be instinctively protective? Casey finally released her grip on Dede and looked into her eyes. The young teen reached over to wipe the tears from Casey's face. Sonofabitch. Dede smiled. "It's okay, don't cry."

Casey dabbed her eyes with a napkin and smiled. "Yeah, I know. I used to never let it show either. It's like a numbness, you know?"

Dede nodded.

"Thank you for telling me all of this. We really wanna try to do something about some of it at least."

"It's okay."

"It's not. It's really not anywhere close to okay. But we are going to do something that will maybe prevent it from happening to someone else."

"Okay."

Casey hugged her again. "Okay."

Week Two

"His name is Clement Childs," McAfee told them over breakfast as all three of them devoured the chicken and waffles special. "He's a garden variety scumbag who sells young girls to rich guys. My boys in the sex crimes division have had him on their radar for years now. They've put him away twice, Once for promoting prostitution and once for felony assault. Some john that refused to pay up."

"So what's his tie to Nash?" Douglas asked as he poured on more syrup.

"There most likely isn't one. Those big spenders in Atlanta want their girls fresh faced and healthy. After being force fed drugs for months they start to look worn out and sickly. Then they usually sell them off to street pimps. It's pretty common for them to change hands multiple times. Especially the younger girls."

Casey ate in silence, which was more than unusual for her. Douglas and McAfee exchanged a quick look.

"You okay kid?" Douglas asked her.

Casey looked up from her food and nodded. At least she still had that appetite he thought. "I know this one is troubling. Nobody likes hearing the details of something like this."

"They're all troubling," she answered. "People are such shit. Everywhere you turn they are just plain shit."

"Hey listen," McAfee took a sip of his coffee. "I know cops that delivered babies in the backseat of cars along the road. Fire fighters who saved parents from dying while their kids watched. There are lots of solid people out there who care and wanna help."

"Like you," Douglas agreed. "Both of you. I mean hell, Mac's retired and he's still out here fighting the good fight with us."

"It just seems so crappy," she put her fork down and looked at them. "What's wrong with these guys that would do that to a fourteen year old?"

She was asking why she had been a victim, as much as she was about Dede, and they knew it.

"Since the dawn of time," McAfee answered before taking a big bite of waffle. "All we can do is keep catching them."

Since McAfee's former colleagues were going to check into all of Clement Child's known associates there wasn't much else they could do without more information. Casey pulled Douglas' car to the curb in front of Carly's apartment building and only waited a couple minutes before Dede came down wearing her new outfit. She climbed in looking happy and it broke Casey out of her funk. "You brought it?"

"Yup," Dede answered. "I wore it under my clothes."

"Cool, me too. To the beach we go!"

The ride out to Tybee island was beautiful. Miles of peaceful flowing seagrass and pools of water beckoned you forward toward the sea, with the occasional turtle bringing the light traffic to a halt as he sauntered from one side of the road to the other. It wouldn't be warm enough to swim, but the two girls had worn their swimsuits under their clothes and planned to spend a couple hours tanning and eating some of the best seafood to be found in the southeast. Here and there a home would appear off in the distance, rising high on stilts in case of seasonal flooding, accented with bright white bahama style shutters and flying American flags from massive poles. Their wrap around porches were often as big as the houses themselves, displaying colorful outdoor furniture and maybe even a hammock or two.

Tybee was its own entity and yet still considered part of Savannah. It was close enough for a quick ride out to spend an hour or so and yet felt like it was remote, especially this time of the year. Many of the beach cottages, motels and

B&B's were closed up for the winter, with just a few still open for the families that wanted to spend their holidays on the beach. It was the same with the restaurants, the majority being closed but the ones that catered to the locals, which were always the best ones, were still open. Casey had called ahead and a place called 'The surf Shack' was open all day and offered clam boats, chowder, fried shrimp, and what they claimed were the best conch fritters to be found anywhere along the Atlantic coast. They stopped there first, ordering one of each of these dishes to go and taking their bag full of red and white take out containers and a couple of sweet teas straight across the road to North beach.

It was about seventy degrees outside, warm for this time of year but with the cool Atlantic breeze blowing in it felt more like sixty. They abandoned the bathing suit idea quickly, laying out their blanket to sit and enjoy their food while they watched the waves crash instead. There were only a few other people around, most further down the beach scouting for shells or jogging. One man was using a metal detector to search for treasure, no doubt hoping to find some old coin from an ancient shipwreck. Casey commented that she hoped he found it. She liked it when people found what they were searching for. She had, and there was no better feeling in the world. She pointed out toward the sea. "Look at that ship way out there."

Dede squinted her eyes. "Oh yeah. What do you think they're doing?"

"Probably a freighter of some kind I guess. It has to be pretty big for us to spot it from here."

"These shrimp are so good."

"I know, girl. Try the fritters, they're deadly."

They sat in satisfied peacefulness for a while, entranced by the soft waves and the outstanding clams that seemed to melt in their mouths. Now and then a seagull would swoop down a little closer, waiting for one of them to drop their guard and hold their food in an unprotected position. They were quick thieves, experienced and wholly dedicated to their mission. The girls were too smart for them today.

"So, I guess I should tell you more about Clem and what happened."

"Whenever you're ready," Casey answered.

"I wasn't allowed out after the night that Clem came into my room. He was around all the time and I'm sure they knew that if I got outside I would run. Each day he'd make me do something...else. Telling me guys want you to do this and some want you to do that. It went on like that for about two weeks or so, just him at that point, and the girls didn't even speak to me much anymore. Bella wouldn't even look me in the eye. Then one night things changed again.

Dede had been in her room watching the t.v. She'd hoped to see her own face pop up on the news, an emergency news conference from the cops about a missing fourteen year old girl that the whole world needed to be watching out for. But that never happened. The news was more concerned about what happened in the congress that day or who was being investigated for corruption. Nobody cared about some small town girl from nowhere Mississippi that wasn't worth nuthin' to nobody. She wondered if her Mama was even looking for her. Had she even made a couple phone calls or asked around town? Did she call the useless Chief of police or ask some of the local men to head out of town a ways and check to see if she was walking? Did she question Dennis about if he saw her that morning before he left for work? No doubt he lied like a rug about it.

This particular evening she was watching real housewives of Atlanta, sipping on a can of diet coke and eating a twizzler, when Clem came in and motioned for her to hand over the can and candy bag. "Get up, brush your teeth, comb your hair and put on that cheerleader outfit I got for you."

"What for?" she asked nervously.

"You trying to get hit? Just do it."

She'd obeyed, so used to the harsh discipline by now that she didn't want any more of it. She'd do what the freak wanted and hopefully he'd be done with whatever it was really fast. But when she came back out of the bathroom dressed in the outfit he looked more disinterested than usual.

"A friend of mine wants to meet you," he mumbled. "And you better remember to be on your best behavior and mind your manners. I promise you I'll tear you up if you embarrass me. You do whatever he asks you to do. Got it?"

She nodded, and he left her room. She began to pace nervously back and forth across her room, waiting for the worst.

"You wanna tell me why Malone has the Mercedes and we're stuck with this piece of crap rental?" McAfee complained.

"You have to be twenty-five to be on the rental agreement and Casey's only twenty," Douglas answered without lowering the binoculars. They were half a block down from Conrad Nash's local office, waiting for...well, anything.

"You could've just kept her off the paperwork. How're they gonna know?"

"It would void the insurance if there was an accident."

McAfee grunted. "They're out on the beach eating lobster and we're stuck with this stale crap." He looked at his deli sandwich with disgust before taking another bite. Douglas smiled. "You'll make it through this."

They had spent the morning following Nash from his townhouse to his office and were now just...sitting. They weren't exactly sure what they were waiting for, but were both just hoping for some little morsel of something that might lead them to something bigger. Sometimes this was how these things went, sitting in a car and waiting for somebody to do something stupid.

"You can lower the binoculars," McAfee went on. "We can see the door pretty clearly."

"I'm looking at faces. Maybe somebody will stand out."

"Right. Maybe the head of the Sinaloa cartel will walk in the front door of Nash's office."

Douglas knew he was right. He lowered the binoculars and grabbed his can of now lukewarm soda. "You're right about the seafood though. That would sure hit the spot right now."

"So you and Malone planning on continuing your trip when this gets wrapped up?"

"No. We want to be home for Christmas and she needs to be back in school the second week of January."

"What you getting her for Christmas?"

Douglas chuckled. "Man you must be bored."

Mcafee grinned. "Guilty."

"I was thinking of a large screen for her room."

"Sweet. A fifty?"

"I think so, yeah. You think bigger?"

"I like the fifty."

"Yeah, me too."

Nash suddenly exited the front door of his office building and they both sat up straight. McAfee looked at his watch. "Lunch meeting probably."

"I guess we'll find out."

Douglas started the car as Nash climbed into the back seat of his waiting Cadillac Escalade and pulled out slowly to follow behind. The black SUV made its way through new town traffic and out toward the Interstate with Douglas maintaining a safe distance behind. It turned off the country highway a few miles before reaching ninety-five and headed toward a small industrial area, but once they had reached it they just passed right on by, heading out into a sparsely inhabited area on the other side. They made a series of turns down badly maintained asphalt roads before pulling into a neighborhood of older, rough looking small houses. The vehicle came to a stop in front of a two story frame house with peeling gray paint and an overgrown lawn. Nash climbed out of his vehicle and headed inside.

Douglas had pulled over into some high weeds beside the road, hoping that they would help to hide the fact that the vehicle was fairly new.

"Turns out letting the kid take the Mercedes was a good idea," McAfee commented. "We would've stuck out like a sore thumb."

"That's for sure."

"Nuthin' out here but rusty lawnmowers and crystal meth."

"And whatever Nash is here for."

"Yeah. I think we both know what that is."

The two men sat for nearly half an hour when they spotted a young girl, fifteen at the most, approach the house on foot and let herself inside.

"She damn sure wasn't dressed for school," McAfee frowned.

"No, that's for sure. My guess is they're not just using these girls for the big spenders. Some of them might be working the local streets."

"Which puts them in even more danger."

"Anybody who'd do this to a child doesn't much care."

"I'll make sure the local cops get this address."

"Wait till Nash is gone. If we catch him up in some local stuff he may slip away from the bigger charge."

Casey and Dede had finished their lunch and had decided to take a walk along the shore. They'd left their shoes on their blanket and allowed the softly lapping water to come in and out over their feet.

"Gosh I'm stuffed," Casey rubbed her belly.

"I know," Dede laughed. "I can't believe we ate all that."

"Girl, I need to lose like fifty pounds after this trip."

Dede looked Casey up and down and smiled. "Yeah, you would disappear."

"Well, at least five."

"What will happen once they find out who took me?"

"They'll wish they hadn't. I'll tell you that much."

Dede nodded. "Well, I'll tell you some more of what happened if you want."

That first time hadn't been as bad as some of the ones that would come after. He had spoken to Dede kindly, been gentle even. But none of that had stopped him from doing what he had come there to do. It hadn't been at all violent, as it had been with Dennis and Clem, but then again she had been too afraid to try fighting. She knew that all that would have done is to invite Clem's rage, and in the end the middle aged guy who'd come to see her would have had his way anyhow. He had told her she was pretty, that she was very special. He thought she was stupid. He was a rapist, a child rapist. He was a pathetic, fat, balding rapist who would never be with a pretty young woman unless he did exactly this. He could pretend during the act that they were in a relationship, that she cared about his whispered compliments. But when it was done and he saw the revulsion in her eyes the reality of his pathetic reality would come driving home.

He was the first of many in that apartment. Sometimes even two in one night. Sometimes their demands were spoken softly, almost shyly. But as time passed by she grew to recognize that seeming vulnerability for the farce that it was. They were evil. Every single last one of them. Some were just more outwardly rough and horrible than the others. It went on for months. Wear this and do that. After a while she became almost numb to it. Or at least tried to be. She'd be allowed here and there to go out for a bit with Bella, maybe to a store or for some fast food. She'd been warned about what would happen if she ran. The consequences when he caught her. And she was one hundred percent convinced that he would catch her. He knew the city. Knew the routes in and out. He had connections with the cabbies and uber drivers. Maybe even some of the cops. There was very little chance of a successful run.

Clem had never forced himself on her again after that first week. Bella said he didn't even like girls. It was just to exert his dominance over her. Let her know that he owned her in every single way. Now and then he'd slap her around if a customer claimed to be unhappy. The other girls said that was usually bullshit, a way to get out without paying full price. Clem would tolerate some roughness but any time a guy crossed the line into violence toward her he would beat them worse than the girls. She knew better than to think it was because he cared for her. He just didn't want his merchandise damaged. He offered her drugs but never forced her. Bella said the girls who wouldn't cooperate were forced. She said their faces would become worn out like old ladies and they would waste away until they looked like they were dying. Then one day they would just be gone. Nobody dared to ask where.

Several months passed by before Clem told her she would be going into rotation. She didn't know what that meant but he seemed unhappy about it. One night he told her to pack up her stuff in a suitcase and escorted her downstairs and out to the street where a van full of other girls was waiting. One of them was told to get out and go with Clem and she was told to get in and buckle up. The two men in the front seats told the six girls that they could talk if they wanted to and a couple of them did a little bit.

They talked about music and movies and what they liked to eat. Dede sat in silence and watched the city lights fade away as they entered first into a rural area and then eventually into the city of Athens. The trip was only an hour and a half, but she had enjoyed the freedom of it as if she'd been away on vacation.

They had arrived at a house this time, in a high end neighborhood with vast lawns between the properties. The place was massive, seven bedrooms she would soon learn, with a media room, gym, and even a swimming pool. They could enjoy all of it as long as they did their "work." It was two girls to a room, entertaining alone unless a customer or a couple of guys asked for it to be otherwise. The place was beautiful. Even the Atlanta apartment could not compare to this. The furniture and artwork were unlike anything she'd been exposed to before. She couldn't begin to fathom the cost. Were it not for her circumstances she would have considered herself lucky to live in such a place. She almost wished she could send some pictures home to her Mama.

A ship's horn sounded off a short way in the distance and the two girls waved madly even though they were certain it hadn't been saying hello to them. Casey took Dede by the hand and they began to walk back the way they had come. Dede had been talking for about an hour and they had strolled a good distance from their blanket. It was four in the afternoon, and it would start to get dark in an hour or so. Casey wanted to make the drive back before it got too black.

"Have you called your Mama since you escaped?"

"No. I'm afraid to."

"Why?"

"What if she's ashamed of me?"

"I'm sure she's nothing but worried."

"I dunno. I ran away. What if she thinks it's all my fault?"

"You need to tell her the reason. She needs to know what happened. You know she loves you."

Dede shrugged and Casey changed the subject. "You think at all about what you'd like to do with your life now?"

"What d'you mean?"

"Like, do you wanna finish school? Is there something you think you'd like to do for a living someday?"

Dede looked out over the vast sea. It was evident that the thought of having a whole new life hadn't occurred to her yet.

They made it back to the blanket, stopping for just a brief few moments to let the surf run over their toes before gathering up their things and heading back to the car. The parking lot was nearly empty now. An older model compact car was off a little ways and a black van was parked up nearer to the entrance by the road. Casey folded the blanket neatly and placed it in the trunk before the two climbed into the front and headed out. She was only a couple minutes down the road before noticing in her rearview mirror that the van had also left the parking area and was back a short distance behind them. Ordinarily that wouldn't mean anything, but right now it was triggering a strong sense of danger. She tried not to be too obvious about it but failed. Dede looked at her before turning to look out the back window. "What's wrong?"

"Probably nothing." Casey kept checking every couple seconds.

"Oh my god. Are they following us?"

"Grab my cell out of my bag would you please."

Dede grabbed the phone and Caset told her to dial Douglas and put it on speaker.

He answered immediately. "You two on your way back?"

"I think we might have a problem."

"What is it?"

"A black van. It followed us out of the beach parking lot and it's been behind us for about five minutes. They had a couple opportunities to pass and I slowed way down to see if they would but no."

"Okay, where are you right now?"

"On sixteen about twenty minutes out. We just passed the tiny market."

"The one with the painted boat out front?"

"Yeah."

"Okay. Mac's contacting the local cops and asking them to get to you. We're hopping in the car as we speak to head your way."

"It might be nothing."

"Then no harm no foul. Let's hope so."

Casey stayed on the line with the two men, providing updates on where they were. About five minutes further down the road she spotted a police cruiser beside the road.

"I see a cop."

"Good. Pull in next to him, they're waiting on you."

As she pulled off into the small dirt area she saw the van suddenly stop before doing a three point turn and heading back the other direction. It was too far off to try and get a tag number. She rolled down her window to speak to the officer who made the smart decision to remain with the girls rather than pursue the van. After all, driving down the road was not a crime and maybe it was all perfectly innocent.

Douglas and Mac flew in beside them a few minutes later clearly irking the local officer who began to lecture them about their speed. McAfee flashed a badge and his expression alone quieted the man instantly. The girls climbed out and Douglas gave Casey a quick hug. "You did good."

"It may have been nothing."

"Maybe. But from here on out we assume that they know who we all are and also, Dede, that they know where you're staying. We need to make some changes."

McAfee followed them back into the city but there was no further sign of the black van. Douglas drove his own car, letting Casey settle her nerves from the frightening experience. One of the things that Douglas knew for sure about Casey was that her instincts were generally spot on. If she sensed danger then there most likely was danger, and this was going to change the way they handled things from here on out. They phoned Carly over the car speaker and told her about what had happened and that they were going to take Dede into their own protection for the immediate future. Douglas also suggested that Carly herself find somewhere else to stay for a few days and she agreed to crash on a friend's sofa just in case. What had been their plan? Douglas wondered to himself. They knew it would be far too risky to put Dede back to work. Would they have murdered her? No doubt they'd done it before. Sex traffickers were not known to have any boundaries as far as their business was concerned. If they were grabbing her here, though, they must have planned to bring her someplace close by. They needed to know more about the Savannah operation. They needed to know more about Conrad Nash.

The four of them met Carly at her apartment and the men waited as Casey helped Dede and Carly pack up what they'd need.

"You think they were on to just kill her?" Douglas asked.

"Bet. They can't have this girl jus' runnin' around free. She knows too much about all of it. We need to get that info from her quick though cause I guaranfuckintee you that they are already fixin' to shut down every location she knows about. If they weren't onto you and I already then they damn sure were when they saw Casey had a line to the cops."

"We'll have to push her as soon as we get back to the motel."

"And we need to move from there ourselves."

"How much time do you think we have?"

"Not much at all. But they have to move those girls and their clothes and stuff. There's no way they're gonna let their money go like that. That gives us a little bit."

"So what's the plan?"

"We push for whatever locations she's got here locally and I'll get on it with the locals while y'all pack up all our shit at the motel and make the move. Right now I'm sure it's all hands on deck for them so there's a good chance nobody's watching us. Just assume there is anyway just in case."

They were out the door within ten minutes, Carly headed off in one direction while Douglas, McAfee, Casey and Dede headed back to the motel. McAfee had cautioned Carly to repeatedly make turns and check her mirrors for a tail. Chances were that they'd abort any attempts to grab Dede and move on to whatever their plan B was. But you could never be sure. Anger often made people do stupid things and allowing this sixteen year old girl to put a financial hurting on them had to be a hard pill to swallow. They would need to move quickly if they wanted to have even a remote prayer of rescuing some of the girls before they were moved. The Savannah PD was preparing to move quickly as soon as McAfee gave them the info they'd need. He and Douglas had decided against any mention of Conrad Nash for right now. The State Rep was a good friend of law enforcement and they might not like the allegation. They were taking a risk as it was that some of the cops might actually be connected to Nash's criminal activities.

Once they'd reached the motel Douglas and Casey went about the task of packing up their three rooms while

McAfee sat with Dede. He was, after all, the most experienced in these matters having been a cop for nearly forty years and a major crimes detective for thirty of them. He was feeling every moment of that time in his bones these days, but was still sharp as a tack and with the instincts to match. A week would rarely pass by without one of Atlanta's finest calling to ask him about some case he'd worked, or for advice on how to handle some situation or other. The fact that he was now retired didn't seem to change the way he operated in the least. He still flashed his badge and still gave out orders. Since he was big, broad and mean looking, people rarely questioned him.

McAfee smiled softly at Dede. That was always the hard part for him. It wasn't that he lacked in either compassion or concern, he just didn't exactly fit the image of a victim advocate. Douglas was much softer in his manner and Malone was coming into her own and gaining lots of valuable experience. The kid had actually become an asset, though he'd never admit it to her, and for all their back and forth jabs he'd developed a soft spot for her. She was smart and scrappy. She kinda reminded him of himself when he was young. He was already in the academy at her age, ready to set the world on fire. He'd taken a few good hits himself by then. Nothing like she'd gone through but tough times just the same. His Dad had been a cop too. He was also a mean, violent drunk who enjoyed the tears of his wife and kids. It wasn't his father's career that had inspired him to become a cop but his father's abusive ways. He'd grown up hating him, hating bullies. Hating every single loathsome mutherfucker who'd put his hands on a weaker person in that way.

The first time Lloyd had seen his Dad become violent toward his mother was when he was about seven. It had probably happened lots before then but either his Dad had hidden it well or he'd just been too young to remember. She'd come home from the grocery store with the wrong kind of beer and though she'd tried desperately to explain that they'd been out of stock his rage was quick and unforgiving. He'd beaten her with the buckle of his belt until she was in a fetal position on the kitchen floor bloodied and terrified. Lloyd and his brother had tried several times to intercede and protect her but his dad was an easy two-fifty. Lloyd had a tooth knocked out and some nasty looking bruises for his efforts. They'd clung to their mother on the floor, the three of them crying while his father laughed and called them three useless little bitches.

McAfee became aware that Dede was quietly waiting for him to ask her his questions. They'd taken seats at the little table in his room near the front picture window so he could watch for any possible approaching threat. He saw Douglas and Casey loading their bags into the trunk before quietly entering his room and beginning to pack up his things.

"Dede," he began. "Because of what happened earlier with the van we'd like to try and move quickly and maybe be able to rescue some of the other girls that are being kept in town here."

"Yessir."

"Good. So what I'd like you to do is try and remember any place you may have stayed once they moved you from Athens to Savannah. Do you remember an address maybe? Or a sign for a street or neighborhood? Was it a house and if so was it close by to a park or store maybe?

Dede remembered the day she'd been moved from Athens. She hadn't been there all that long. Not even as long as the Atlanta apartment. Her time there had been a bit easier in some ways then it had in Atlanta. She enjoyed being able to use the pool and interact with the other girls more than she had before. There were twelve girls in the Athens mansion. She'd learned that the house had been nine thousand square feet and every inch of it was amazing. There were four regular guys who'd take turns staying with them, and they'd give you at least a half hour notice if you had a date coming. A couple of the guys were actually very good cooks and they'd even take a request here and there. Other times they'd order pizza or Chinese and let you choose whatever you'd like. They wanted you to be happy they'd say, but what they really wanted was cooperation without any headaches. Since defying any of them would lead to a beating she'd decided to just do as she was told and try to block out the worst of it.

She'd been a couple of months into the routine of the new house when she was told she'd be rotating once more. She'd assumed she'd be delivered back to Clem in Atlanta but ended up in an old plantation house outside of the city of Savannah. Though the property was pretty the house itself was rather run down when compared to the Athens mansion. It was in need of a paint job by at least a dozen years and the long dirt driveway approaching the house was invaded by weeds and filled with potholes that no one seemed to care about fixing. The vast lawns were shaded by old oaks and magnolias leaving patches of soil where no sunlight was able to peek through. It looked like the lawn maintenance was a quick, half-assed attempt to keep the higher grass away from the immediate perimeter of the home, most likely to keep the field mice away.

The men who operated the house were different as well. They were nowhere near as accommodating and couldn't give a crap what you felt like eating. They also regularly had their way with the girls, something the others had never done, at least not to Dede or any of the girls she was with. They were rough about it too, seeming to enjoy inflicting as much hurt as they could without leaving a mark. The customers didn't like the girls being bruised up or looking like they were forced to be there. Though you'd have to be plain simple to not know that a bunch of young girls were not choosing to have sex with multiple fat, bald men every day. She supposed they were just lying to themselves so that they wouldn't have to admit that they were, in fact, rapists.

It had been summertime and as was common there wasn't a breeze to be found in the whole south. When she wasn't with a date she'd like to sit under one of the shade trees and watch for the rabbits who'd poke out from the tall grass every now and then to see what she was up to. One even came up close enough for her to hand feed him a sliver of carrot from her plastic baggie that she'd brought out for her snack. The men were more watchful here but once they knew you weren't fixin' to run they'd pretty much let you wander about as long as you stayed fairly close to the house in case they booked you for a date. Every couple of days they'd have you dress in a different outfit and pose in certain ways and then post your pics online for the perverts to shop through. They always said she was eighteen but the girls had told her back in Atlanta that these guys only dealt in younger girls and all the pedophiles knew it. They'd also have the girls fix each other's hair in different ways each week to make it look like they had more girls available than they actually did.

McAfee jotted down a few notes on his pad as Dede offered up a few details that might help.

"Did you happen to catch a number on the house? Maybe see what was close by before you pulled into the driveway?"

"I don't recall seeing any number. It was a country road and we got there in the dark so I really don't know if anything was around."

"Did you ever hear any noises? Maybe traffic passing by or a train?"

"No Sir. Nothing like that."

"Tell me about the house itself. Was there anything unique about it? You grew up in the country. Was there a barn or anything that'd make you think it was used for dairy or produce anytime recently?"

"Not that I could see. No barn. No stables or fruit boxes or nothing."

"What about the furniture? Was it new or had it been there forever?"

"It was old. Some of it pretty rickety so you couldn't use it no more."

"How about artwork on the walls? Any paintings maybe of what the place used to look like in its heyday?"

"Just a couple old barn paintings and such."

"That maybe used to be there?"

"I don't guess so. They were in the wide open and there were too many trees at the house for that."

"Anything else stand out?"

Dede thought for a moment. "There was a picture in a frame over the fireplace that one of the girls told me was the governor lady."

"Teresa Jacobs? Our Governor?"

"I dunno. Maybe. It was her and some other dude."

"Another dude? Her husband?"

"No clue. One of the girls said he was one of the bosses."

"The bosses?"

"Yessir."

McAfee snapped his finger at Casey and motioned for her to bring him over his laptop. He flipped it open and typed quickly before showing a photo to Dede.

"Is this the boss-man in the photo?"

Dede squinted to see it better. "Yup, that's him."

McAfee nearly jumped out of his seat. "Douglas, it's Nash!"

Douglas came over to the table. "You sure Dede?"

"Yessir. I'm sure."

"Casey, look up property records for the County and see what's listed for Conrad Nash."

"Okay but there's probably bunches of pictures of the two of them together. He's a State Representative."

"Yeah, but sometimes where there's a whiff of smoke..."

Casey typed and clicked and typed some more. "Okay. There's about ten different Nash's listed as property owners and three of them are Conrad's."

"Mac, is there a middle initial on his bio there on your screen?"

McAfee checked. "Yeah, P."

"Got it. Conrad Patrick Nash. There's, let me see, six properties. The townhouse we know about, some commercial property, some house that's valued at only like forty grand."

"That's the one we followed him to," Douglas peered over her shoulder.

"And this place that's zoned agricultural. Valued at eight hundred fifty."

"Address?" McAfee answered.

"Number Seven, Old Fork road."

"Enter it into my gps, Malone. I'm gonna use your phone to call this in to the locals."

Once McAfee had headed out to meet up with the cops at the plantation house Douglas, Casey and Dede headed down toward the river before turning West, in the opposite direction from the coast. They'd already been tracked to the beach once and they weren't about to risk it again. Which was unfortunate, Douglas thought, because the distraction would've been good for the girls.They'd decided against any hotels or motels, choosing instead to go with a privately owned three bedroom cottage listed on one of the vacation sites. Casey had found it, booked it and paid for it all from her phone before they'd even arrived. The owner had messaged her back the code for the front door and that there were extra towels in the utility closet and a map to all the sites in the drawer nearest the sink.

"I hope she's got some take out menus in the drawer too," Casey commented quietly.

Douglas smiled. "I'm glad your appetite is still there."

"A girl's gotta eat."

The place was nicer than they'd expected for the price, cedar- sided with some neatly trimmed hedges and a few Christmas decorations hung around the yard for good measure.

"Hey girls, not bad, right?"

"It's really nice, Dede smiled."

Casey looked about suspiciously. I'll reserve judgement till we see the inside."

"But for the price…" Douglas shrugged.

"True. It ain't the ghetto, that's for sure."

The interior of the cottage brought smiles all around. It had been recently updated, with a small but inviting kitchen and modern bathrooms that were so clean they sparkled. There were three bedrooms, one for the girls to share and one for each of the men. Outside the back door was a deck that also appeared to be new, running the full length of the rear of the cottage and offering Adirondack chairs and a couple loungers which overlooked the wooded property. The living room was comfortable and decorated in traditional cottage style with a mission style sofa and comfortable, overstuffed chairs. There was a beautiful stone fireplace with freshly cut wood stacked beside it that would be incredible on cool nights. There were handmade quilts and pillows placed about the room as well as artwork they assumed had been done by local artists. Savannah had a thriving art community and there was a gallery for every possible taste.

Casey and Dede carried their things into their room and went about unpacking. Dede didn't have very much and Casey made a mental note to talk to Douglas about that and see if they could do a little more. The room had two twin beds, each beneath its own window, and a couple of small but cute dressers with a full length mirror in between which Casey loved. Though the room was pine from ceiling to floor to furniture, the lighting was great and the space felt bright and cheerful. There was a small stack of books on a table in the corner and Casey walked over to check them out.

"Stephen King, Nora Roberts, Tami Hoag, oh, check it out...Scary stories to tell in the dark." She held it up for Dede to see. "We're reading this tonight for sure out on the deck."

Dede smiled. "You're a bookworm I take it?"

"Oh I'm a full on book geek, girl."

"I don't read much. Hardly ever really." She turned to see a horrified expression on Casey's face and couldn't help but laugh out loud.

"You know we're gonna change that," Casey pointed a finger at her, looking deadly serious."

"Oh, we are?"

"Oh yes. We definitely are."

Douglas sat on the sofa and found Sammy's name in his phone contacts. He pushed it and waited for her to pick up.

"What you got for me Powell?"

"Hey boss lady. Just checking in with an update."

"Y'all got somewhere safe?"

"Yeah, vacation cottage just outside of town. It's pretty nice actually."

"Glad to hear it. When am I getting my story?"

"Well Mac's with the cops now and they should be hitting Nash's plantation house as we speak."

"Well I hope they find something because a teenage prostitute's word against a State Senator's ain't gonna get us nowhere but maybe fired."

"Trafficking victim."

"I know, I get it. It still is what it is."

"Yeah, I know. She's a sweet kid."

"How's Malone doing with her?"

"Oh, Casey's a natural. Instant rapport."

"I need Conrad Nash's head, Douglas. Anything short of that and we have no story and probably a lotta shit from upstairs."

"I know. Believe me we want this guy's ass in the worst way."

"Just remember, you guys are journalists. I need the story. We haven't had a major National since Malone's story."

"I know."

"We need it. The paper needs the paycheck. I need you being interviewed on every television network in the country."

"I know, boss."

"Get it done."

"I will, boss."

"Douglas?"

"Yes Sam?"

"Get it done."

She hung up before he could answer.

McAfee sat in his car and watched as the Savannah PD and the Georgia troopers rushed the front door of the plantation house. It didn't matter though because even from the front seat of the rental car he could tell the place was empty. He saw the first cop in the line try the doorknob and the door opened right up. No need for security when they've already cleared out, he thought. He dialed the number for the Sargeant leading the raid on the house out by the industrial complex.

"Yup, Riggs here."

"Anything?"

"Nada. Sorry Detective. Some empty pizza boxes and a bunch of furniture that ain't worth donating. Nobody in sight."

"Alright. Thanks."

"You got it."

He dialed Casey's number and she picked up immediately. "Hey."

"Yeah. It's a bust."

"Damn."

"Yeah. Try to get me something else to work with. Another location, a name, anything."

"K."

"Right. Hit me back."

He disgustedly tossed the phone over his shoulder into the backseat as one of the Savannah Detectives came back out the door and shrugged. McAfee sighed as he opened the car door and hauled his big frame out of the small rental. He made his way to the front steps and the waiting detective.

"Nuthin?"

"Just an empty house?"

"Signs of drug use? Restraints? Anything?"

"Sorry."

"Damnit."

"We could print though?"

"Yeah, good idea. The bathrooms and kitchen. Maybe we can get some matches on some missing kids."

"Okay. I hope you know what you're doing, brother. Conrad Nash is nobody to play with."

"Yeah, well, too late now. We've got the warrant so let's go for broke."

The young cop made his way back inside and McAfee looked out over the front lawn. It was times like these that made him regret quitting smoking. He spotted a large tree off to the side of the yard and thought maybe it was the one Dede had talked about sitting under. He strolled over and lowered himself down to rest against the massive trunk. The kid was right, it was a peaceful spot. He waited for a few minutes to see if maybe one of the rabbits she had talked about would pop its head out. But when none came around he decided to walk the property and see if anything might stand out. He got to one knee and placed his hands against the tree to push back up to his feet. But before he shoved off he glanced to his left and something caught his eye. In the patchiness of green foliage and sandy colored earth a dark spot lay just beyond the treeline into the woods. He got to his feet and walked over slowly, checking the ground as he walked for anything of possible value. Decades on the job had taught him to be meticulous, to examine anything and everything. When he reached the spot he moved a few taller weeds away with the toe of his shoe and sighed. It was a patch of fresh earth, mounded a slight bit on top and still very fresh. He knelt down and looked closely for anything that might be visible before getting back to his feet and calling back toward the house to a young uniformed trooper.

"Hey! Get a crime scene tech out here!"

Back at the cottage Douglas had asked Casey and Dede to join him in the living room so he could try to possibly gather some new information from Dede. If they could find one active location, anywhere, or even some simple detail that could lead to an arrest, they might be able to shut this whole operation down. The girls sat side by side on the sofa and Douglas faced them from his chair near the fireplace, yellow pad resting on his crossed legs.

"Dede, Did you see or maybe were you just aware of any other location these guys were using in Savannah?"

"No sir. Just the plantation house."

"Okay. How about in Athens? Are you able to give me any idea at all where the mansion was?"

"I don't know the address there. We were only allowed outside in the backyard and it had a high fence."

"On the way there did you see maybe a school or a store or maybe even a lake or pond?"

"It was dark so I really didn't see anything."

"That's probably why they always moved them at night," Casey shook her head.

Douglas thought for a moment. "When you were in the backyard did you happen to notice many planes passing over?"

Dede thought for a moment. "I'm sorry. I really don't think I ever noticed."

Casey took Dede by the hand and smiled. "It's okay. You can only do what you can do. How 'bout we switch gears for a minute. Do you remember much about any of the men that visited you for dates? Did anybody happen to mention their names? Maybe they wore a shirt with a company name on it or some kind of uniform that stuck out?"

Dede sat up a bit. "There was this guy…" She went quiet for a moment as she thought. "He came in a few times and always asked for me. He wore a black polo shirt…"

Casey and Douglas sat on the edge of their seats and waited. Dede closed her eyes trying to remember. When she opened them she spoke with certainty. "Carlton-Chambers Technologies."

Douglas leaned forward with his pad. "That's what it said?"

"Yessir."

"You're certain?"

"Yes."

Douglas nodded to Casey who got up and went quickly into her room for her laptop, coming back moments later and taking her seat back on the sofa as she opened it and began typing.

"Carlton-Chambers Technologies. It looks like some type of high tech security firm. Innovative solutions for an ever changing world. A bunch of other bullshit like that but yeah, security equipment, data protection software, consulting services."

"Any staff photos?" Douglas asked.

"No."

"Okay. Great job Dede. Let me get on the phone to Mac and see if he can get us some. You think you'll be able to spot this guy from a photo?"

"Oh yes. I'll never forget. He was...mean."

Casey put her arm around Dede and Douglas got up to place his call from out back.

It wasn't a body. Thank God for that. But better, it was a stash of records that they probably had every intention of coming back for. They had most likely been afraid to move them in their vehicles for fear that they were too late and might be pulled over by the police. There were about two hundred names, with phone numbers or other contact information, probably for blackmail use if it was ever needed. There were also a couple of computer hard drives, half a dozen fake Georgia driver licenses, two nine millimeter glocks, and three bottles of oxycodone. McAfee's phone rang as he watched the detective's sort through the plastic storage boxes that had been buried. He pulled the phone from his pocket and saw Douglas' name on the screen.

"Yeah."

"We got a company name in Athens where one of Dede's regulars worked."

McAfee was very happy with the news. "Really? Where?"

"Carlton-Chambers technologies. It's high tech security consultation and equipment. No employee photos on their website but Dede says she can ID him if we show her one."

"First name or anything?"

"No. Just the uniform shirt that he wore each time she saw him."

"Security huh? You think maybe he was providing their camera setup in exchange for time with one of the girls?"

"I hadn't thought of that but maybe, yeah."

"So if we get him we can squeeze him for the name of whoever hired him. Maybe get him a deal where he gets out of prison before he's an old man."

"Can you get the Savannah PD to make a call to Athens and see if they can get ID photos from the company? The local cops there might actually know the owner's, being as it's a security firm."

"I'm on it."

"Anything else in the boxes?"

"Just what I texted you. They're still searching."

"Alright, let me know."

Douglas went back inside to find Casey and Dede studying some takeout menus they'd found in a kitchen drawer. He hadn't even noticed how hungry he was himself until he thought about food.

"What looks good?"

Casey looked up. "Everything. Looks like they'll deliver almost anything here."

"Tourist town."

"Yeah. The greek place claims to have the best Moussaka in the south. Comes with side salads and cucumber ranch."

Douglas smiled. "I'm in."

Casey turned to Dede who shrugged. "I never had it but I like to try new things."

"Oh you're gonna love it." Casey grabbed her cell and dialed the number to order as Douglas handed her his credit card.

Detective Ryan Dexter of the Savannah PD sat beside McAfee on the front steps of the plantation house and spoke with the Athens PD. "Right...Okay. We appreciate it y'all. Right, thanks." He hung up and turned to McAfee. "They're getting on it asap. They said they're gonna just run over there so that they feel pressed to give it up quickly. A company like that has to have that stuff handy."

"Good. Between that and all this crap we found we should be on track for something to break soon."

"You sure about Conrad Nash?"

"Well, this is his house."

The detective nodded. "Yeah, but damn."

"I know it."

"So I guess we just wait unless you want me to round up Nash for questioning?"

"Nah, let's not just yet. He don't know we found this stuff. He might figure his boys are too smart for this. But they ain't. So he won't run for the time being."

"He's gotta be nervous."

"Yep. But an 'ol boy like him with that kinda cash is gonna run faster than a scared rabbit if we make a move before we're ready to lock him up."

"What if he just cuts and runs now?"

"He won't. Not with a shot at the Governor's mansion. He's too arrogant for that. He'll wait till we get an arrest warrant. You know the local judges are all gonna tip him off. Then we get to catch him trying to run on top of all the solid evidence. Nah, we'll sit on him but no moves yet."

The Mousaka turned out to be even better than promised. Douglas and the girls had decided to eat out back on the picnic table and enjoy the sixty degree weather. It had been a very long day. Productive though as far as this story was concerned. Between the line on one of Dede's regulars and the assorted incriminating evidence that McAfee had found they were skating toward a possible resolution. Douglas wanted to have a talk with Dede and now seemed to be as good a time as any.

"So, Dede."

She smiled. "Yes sir?"

"You know, we're hopefully gonna have this whole nasty thing wrapped up soon."

"I'll be happy when they are all in jail."

"Me too, love. But, we also need to decide where you go when it's all done. Have you thought any more about calling your Mama?"

Dede lowered her eyes and only shrugged. Casey made eye contact with Douglas before jumping in. "She must be awful worried about you. You said y'all were so close."

"Yes but that was before..."

"I know. But remember your Mama didn't know nuthin about all that. She most likely still don't know."

"I don't even know if she will believe me."

Casey knew the feeling. She knew all the horrible feelings. The worst part of so many abuse stories was that victims tended to be the ones shamed, blamed, or just flat out disbelieved.

"I'll go with you to see her if you want me to."

Dede seemed surprised. "You will?"

"Of course I will. We can tell her the whole story together if you'd like."

"What if she don't want me back?"

"There are other options that we can explore," Douglas answered. "But first I think that talking with your Mama and Casey is a good idea. We need to make sure of course that you'll be safe at home and that she knows what happened to you there."

"Also, therapy is good," Casey added. "It helped me a lot."

"And we can help you with every bit of it," Douglas agreed. "We have lots of resources."

Dede nodded. "Can I sleep on it just for tonight?"

Douglas smiled. "Of course you can, sweetheart. But with things moving so quickly I think making a call tomorrow would be a good idea."

"Yes sir."

"Okay, good then. Now, what did you girls order for our dessert?"

The old plantation house looked far different in the dark than it had in the daytime hours. All of the charm seemed to hide itself away as if frightened the darkness would bring out the true nature of the estate. McAfee had just finished the Big Mac that Detective Dexter had brought back for him when Dexter's phone buzzed.

"Yup?"

"Oh yeah...great news. Hey we appreciate y'all moving so quickly on this. Anytime you need us, okay? Right, thanks again." He hung up and nodded to McAfee. They just e-mailed the company photos to me. Let's go inside and take a look."

"Perfect. I'll forward them right over to Douglas and hopefully we get a name."

"I'm gonna shut down the ground search. I think we found what we're gonna find."

"Agreed."

"I'll keep an officer posted here over-night just in case anybody tries to come back for their stash."

"You ready for one of the biggest busts of your life, Detective?"

"Sign me up brother."

Douglas hund up with McAfee and nodded to Casey.

"Okay," Casey took Dede by the hand and led her back inside to the kitchen table where the lighting would be better. She opened her laptop and slid it over to Douglas who pulled up his email. He typed for a few moments before sliding it back over in front of Casey and Dede.

"So," Casey put her arm around Dede. "There are thirty-six employed in total but only twenty-three are men. I'm gonna pull up their pics and you can just take your time and look through them. There's no hurry okay?"

Dede looked at the photos on the screen.

"You can click on any one you want to see larger," Casey added.

"That's him." Dede pointed.

"Right there?"

"Yes."

"Let me make it bigger. There."

"Yes. That's him."

"Are you sure? Take your time. There's no rush."

"I'm sure. That's him."

Douglas got up and came to peer over their shoulders. "Troy Simmons. Senior system analyst. Looks maybe forty, you think Casey?"

"Yeah, there about."

"Any more information on there about him?"

Casey searched for a minute. "No. There are some bios but only for the executives."

"Alright. Get out of that and try a search for his name in Athens. Anything at all. Public records, criminal history, whatever you can get quick. See if we can grab an address."

Casey got to work and Douglas patted Dede's shoulder. "You okay?"

"A little scared."

Douglas knelt down beside her chair. "Listen, the one promise I will absolutely make you is that we won't leave you alone. You're going to be safe and protected."

"Yes sir."

"Looks like he owns a condo. That's the only Troy Simmons I see in property records," Casey jumped in.

"Okay. Get that to Mac along with his photo. They'll be able to check it against his driver license photo."

"Okay...sent."

Ten minutes later McAfee and Detective Dexter had compared the two photos and had a match.

"Alright then," McAfee smiled. "Now we're cookin' with gas. Can you get back on with Athens PD and tell them we've got our boy."

"Will do. You wanna be there when they question him?"

"If they don't mind. You should too and I'll invite one of my boys from Atlanta out too. Everybody's gonna have a piece of the puzzle on this one and it'll add up to something huge."

"Gotcha."

"Tell them to keep it casual. Invite him to come in the morning for some quick questions regarding a case they're working on."

"Ten sound okay?"

"Yeah. We can head out early and meet with them first. I'm heading out to get some shut eye. I'll meet up with you in the morning. Tell your boys nobody gets anywhere near this house."

It was nearly eleven when McAfee walked in the front door of the cottage. Douglas was relaxing in the living room and working on his laptop. He looked around and nodded.

"This don't look at all bad."

"It's actually very nice."

"Where are the girls?"

"Back deck. Casey is reading some strange book that makes her very happy to Dede."

McAfee smirked as he lowered himself onto the sofa. "Better Dede than me."

"It was a good day my friend."

"You know it brother. I have to admit, I wasn't at all sure this was gonna go anywhere but now…"

"If you guys can get this Troy Simmons to flip on the Athens crew then maybe we get them to give up everybody else."

"That's the plan. I want Nash bad."

"Me too."

McAfee tilted his head back toward the rear of the house. "She call home?"

"She asked to sleep on it tonight but I think she will in the morning. Casey will take her when she's ready."

"Mmm. Well, I'm fixin' to pass the hell out. Where's my bed?"

"Second door down the hall."

McAfee got back to his feet. "I'll be out early. I'll call you as soon as we have anything at all."

"Night."

"Yeah."

Week Three

They pulled out of Savannah at five in the morning. The drive to Athens was about four hours with decent traffic conditions and they wanted an hour cushion to meet with the Athens detectives before they interviewed Troy Simmons. His record had come back clean which was no surprise considering what he did for a living. No security company like that would've touched him if he'd had any convictions. They shot up twenty-five in good time and picked up the interstate out of Augusta. If things looked good on the gps for slow traffic they'd hop off on seventy-eight straight on up into Athens. Detective Dexter was thirty years McAfee's junior, and he sure liked to talk. They'd barely cleared Statesboro before he started wishing he'd driven his own car and met Dexter there. The boy had already jumped from fishing to football, to that one time his buddy dared him to talk to a pretty girl who was now, thank the stars above, his wife. It was nearly as bad as listening to Malone drag on and on about her dumb ass reality shows. Housewives of who gives a shit. Usually she wasn't even talking to him and Douglas, they'd just be forced to listen as she talked to Emma and Sasha on the phone.

There were lots of beautiful places in the world. McAfee had been privileged to see many of them. First in the service and then on family vacations. But the older he got the more he just wanted to stay put in Georgia. He loved it, there was no denying. All these little towns that had weathered the years with relative grace, some better than others of course. Like everywhere in America they had their fair share of closed up storefronts and shuttered factories. The big online retailers had put a hurting on small town U.S.A. from coast to coast. But the small downtown parks and covered bridges still remained. The gazebos all got their fresh coat of white paint year after year and you could get some fresh produce every weekend without having to look too hard. There was an honest mechanic in every town, unless you were a yankee, then there was a ten percent upcharge. Your own fault for not stickin' to the highway on your way to Florida.

At least this kid wasn't talking about the job. Too many guys spent every free moment telling their war stories and inflating just how badass they thought they were. There I was face to face with five gang members blah blah blah. But they were all terrified of me and laid down their weapons just because they saw the serious look on my face and got scared. It was a bad habit that lots of cops shared.

It sounded better than I spent the whole day reading patrol reports and chasing down leads on a serial shoplifter. McAfee had done it too for a while, until he'd interviewed enough rape victims and pulled enough bodies out of cars to realize that the last thing he should be doing when he was off was trying to keep his mind back there at work. His family kept him grounded in reality and what was really important. The close relationship he'd managed to maintain with them gave him something to look forward to in retirement.

But retirement had been postponed by an offer from Douglas Powell. Two weeks left on the job and Powell had walked into his office and sat himself down without waiting for an invitation. Just like he'd been doing for the past twenty years. They hadn't been more than associates at that time, exchanging information back and forth that proved beneficial to both of their careers. Now Powell came bearing an offer. Come work for the Atlanta Daily as their chief investigator. At first he had balked at the idea. Nah, he said, I'm hanging it up. Enough is enough. But Powell had smiled like you would at a dumb shit kid who had no idea what he was talking about. He wouldn't last a week sitting around the house, Powell told him. He was gonna completely lose his mind if he even tried it. Take the pension, plus the new salary, and bank lots of extra cash for when you really do retire he'd said. And after a little thought he admitted that Powell was probably right. He finished his two weeks, took off a month to spend with his kids, and went right back to work again. Only this time it was flashing a PI badge instead of a PD shield.

Here was the thing of it. As a cop his hands were tied in some ways and now as a private citizen they were tied in different ways. He didn't need to read you your rights to question you, didn't need to worry about entrapment or politics, or even making a collar at all. He'd helped Powell and other investigative journalists with numerous cases involving corruption and most recently helped Powell and Malone on a serious case involving the death of young Jeremy Timmons who'd been bullied literally to death. And now here he was in the middle of what might turn out to be one of the biggest cases of his life. Stopping a large scale human trafficking ring would only cement his decision to throw in with Powell for a few years. If he still had the ability to do some good, and he clearly did, then he should keep doing it.

McAfee became aware that Dexter was still talking. "And so that's when I decided to try my hand at bartending part time. The money is good, I meet a lot of cool people, and I get lots of tips that help me on the job."

"Sounds perfect."

"It is."

"How far out are we?"

"Ah, about ten minutes if the gps is right. Sometimes their time estimates aren't the best."

"You're gonna do the interview with them, right?"

"I can only make the request but yeah, hopefully."

"We can't have them screwing this up. This is our shot."

"I gotcha. No worries. I'll handle it."

McAfee actually liked Dexter, which was rare. He barely tolerated most people. But more importantly he trusted him, and felt as comfortable as he could without actually handling it himself. But if he were to be in the room for the interview it might taint any confession and he needed this to be rock solid. The last thing he needed was for some prosecutor to say the cops didn't get any confession, your honor. Some retired prick from Atlanta with no authority whatsoever did. Then anything he might tell them about the other people involved could be straight out the window as well. No sir, Dexter was gonna need to take care of this.

They pulled into the main office for the Athens PD on Lexington road about nine-fifteen. Dexter grabbed the file containing all the info they'd gathered along with the photos of both the buried items they'd recovered as well as photos of the dirt mound before they dug it all up. As they headed for the front door McAfee tapped Dexter on the shoulder and the two men stopped.

"So hey," McAfee winked. Put one of the photos of the mound on the table and be like, so, what do you know about this? The guy will shit himself if he thinks we found a body in the hole."

Dexter grinned. "Now that's a plan."

They gave their names to the desk officer and were promptly escorted back to a conference room. Two Detectives from their major crimes division met them almost immediately. "Morning fellas. I'm Richter...my partner here is Massey."

Dexter smiled. "Dexter and McAfee. Recently retired from Atlanta. He broke this whole thing."

The men shook hands all around.

"McAfee," Massey said. "You were involved in that Casey Malone thing right?"

"That's right."

"You're the one that put her away."

"Right."

"And then you helped get her back out."

"Also right."

"That's funny."

"If you say so."

The men took their seats and went over the case in as much detail as they could before the desk officer came back to inform them that Troy Simmons had arrived for his interview. Dexter patted McAfee on the shoulder as he was shown into the observation room to watch the interview through the glass. "Don't worry brother. We got this."

"He can't walk outta here without giving it up," McAfee answered. "Or else Conrad Nash will be history."

"I know it."

McAfee whispered, "You trust these guys?"

Dexter looked around quickly for anyone who might be able to overhear. "I don't get a bad vibe."

"No, me either."

"But lots of cops love Nash. We talked about how that might be a problem."

"You have somebody sitting on Nash just in case right?"

"Oh yeah. He ain't going nowhere."

McAfee watched the detectives through the glass and listened through the speaker as they kept things very casual, smiling and shaking hands as they thanked Simmons for coming in to help them out on this. Richter and Massey sat directly across from the suspect and Dexter sat at the end of the small interview table closest to Simmons. He immediately took the lead as the men had agreed to earlier.

"So thanks again Mister Simmons. We appreciate this."

"Sure guys. We always like to help out the police. Please call me Troy."

"Great, so Troy, We're working this case that involves several jurisdictions and at least here, locally, your company's security equipment was being used by our suspects."

"Oh...I'm sorry to hear that."

"Well, what can you do right?"

Troy smiled. "Yeah, right."

"Anyways, it's some hardcore stuff, Troy. Sex trafficking."

The corner of Troy's mouth twitched just the slightest bit, but all three detectives caught it as did McAfee from the other side of the glass.

"Oh my god."

"Yeah."

"That's horrible." Troy shifted in his seat.

"Underage girls," Dexter added without breaking eye contact.

Simmons tried to hold his gaze but needed to lower his eyes or else betray his own panic and start trembling. "That's...that's really…"

"It's life in prison."

Troy began to shift about in his seat, hardly making eye contact with the detectives at all.

"Tell me about Dede, Troy."

Simmons was no longer able to hide his fear. His hands began to visibly shake and he kept his gaze down into his lap. Dexter pulled the photo of the dirt mound from his folder and laid it on the table in front of him. "Tell me about this."

Simmons darn near flew out of his chair. "Wait! I didn't kill her!"

"Kill who?" Dexter asked softly.

"Dede!"

"Look, Troy. We're all in the same business practically. Let us help you out with this. We don't think you killed her either."

"I didn't!"

"When did you see her last?"

"A couple months back or so."

"Alive?"

"Yes! Alive! I swear!"

"Okay, cards on the table cause this is serious for you and we want you off the hook, okay?"

"Yes, anything sir."

"Good. So you did sleep with her?"

"Yes but I thought she was eighteen."

"Who said she wasn't?"

Troy looked positively terrified. "Sir...I…"

"Look, Troy, come on now. We have more than the video from your company. We have phone recordings, records...the requests you made. Take the hit for what you did boy, not what you didn't do."

Simmons looked like a man on the verge of a breakdown. He began sweating profusely even though the station kept the temperature at a cool seventy throughout the entire building. He was wringing his hands nervously and Dexter thought for a moment that the man might even cry. It was very clear that Simmons knew very well that Dede was not eighteen.

"Come on now boy, let us help you out here."

Troy finally made eye contact. "I want immunity!"

The three detectives couldn't help but laugh out loud which seemed to shake Simmons up even worse.

"Troy, listen now. We're going to help you out as much as we can. Recommend a lighter sentence for your cooperation and all that. But we don't need it. We got you either way. The only question you need to be asking yourself is how long you wanna go down for. And for what.

"I didn't kill her I swear!"

"Tell us who was holding her. We need names. All of them."

Twenty minutes later Dexter walked into the observation room and gave McAfee a wink. "That's how we Savannah boys handle shit."

McAfee smiled. "You did good. The Athens fellas did good just stayin' quiet and letting you run the ball."

"So we have three names. No Conrad Nash though I'm afraid."

"That makes sense." McAfee finished off his cup of coffee. "He stays in Savannah most of the time I'm sure except when the legislature's meeting in Atlanta."

"So Richter and Massey know two of the guys that Simmons named. Both of 'em are local pimps who obviously got bumped up a notch working for Nash. They are heading out to scoop them up so we can hopefully question them before we leave."

McAfee nodded toward the glass. "Did he piss himself in there?"

"Damn near but who cares? This ain't our house."

They'd all enjoyed take out the evening before but now it was one in the afternoon and the girls were getting hungry. Douglas thought about getting some groceries delivered but decided that they'd all benefit from stepping out just a little bit. He loaned Dede his Braves ball cap and Casey gave her a pair of sunglasses so that she wouldn't be as easily recognized. Douglas was nearly one hundred percent certain though that the men involved in Dede's imprisonment were long gone. He wondered if Nash himself was beginning to panic yet. At what point would the high profile politician make a break for it and give up the life of privilege he'd built here in Savannah?

They made their way down to river street and managed to find a rare parking space on the cobblestone road. He surprised Casey and Dede by ushering them to an elevator and upstairs to a rooftop restaurant called Charlie's on the Savannah, with gorgeous views of the river and the historic streets below. They chose a relatively private table where Dede could sit with her back toward the other patrons while Doulglas did the opposite to keep a watchful eye on everything. Casey was so delighted by the menu that it made him smile. Anything that made her happy made him smile.

"Y'all! They got a lunch platter with shrimp, crab cakes and grouper fingers. Plus hushpuppies and white cheddar mac and cheese!" She looked up from her menu fully expecting to see her excitement mirrored back at her.

"That sounds so good," Dede nodded.

"You know I'm in," Douglas agreed. "So three platters it is."

The food was as amazing as they figured it would be. You wouldn't last long in the Savannah food scene unless you could deliver the very best. The competition was fierce but with so many visitors there was enough for all the eateries to survive as long as they continued to please. These days one bad online review could put a major hurting on nearly any business. While they ate, Douglas filled them in on McAfee's progress in Athens. Dede seemed to get a bit quiet and Casey put her arm around her. "You're safe now. It won't be long till they get them all."

"I know," she smiled back. "It's just..I dunno. It's kinda dumb but he wasn't the worst of them. Now that I know his name and stuff he's just a regular guy."

"He made his choices," Douglas reassured her. "He knew what he was doing and regardless of how badly his own life may have been going he had no right to exploit an underage girl. Probably multiple girls. The only victims here are you and the other girls they took advantage of."

Casey was deep in thought as she examined the dessert menu. The choice was clearly a difficult one for her and the waitress, who'd been waiting very patiently, made a suggestion. "We have a sampler platter with a little bit of everything that y'all can share."

Casey looked as if she'd been handed a wonderful gift and Douglas laughed. "I think that sounds like a winner."

The young woman took the menu and headed back toward the kitchen.

"So Dede honey, are you ready to talk to your Mama?" Douglas asked.

Dede shrugged. "I'm nervous, but yeah."

"She's gonna be so happy to hear from you girl," Casey reassured her. "And when we get the all clear then you and I will go see her together."

After sampling some of the best desserts they'd ever tried in their lives they decided to go for just a little bit of a car ride around town just to get out for a bit. Savannah was truly a gorgeous city, so rich in history and culture and architecture. They passed by Chippewa square which was made famous by the bench scenes in the movie Forest Gump. They cruised by Forsyth park with its famous fountain and beautiful, shaded walking paths. And though Douglas hesitated for a few moments, he gave in to Casey's request to stop by one of the smaller neighborhood book and coffee shops where she managed to find the latest dark fantasy novel that she'd seen reviewed online. He found himself quite pleased as well with the outstanding coffee the little shop offered. He grabbed three cups to go along with a bag of fresh ground for the cottage. Casey snuck four brownies onto the counter just as the jovial counter-lady checked them out. The girl could pack it away for a little thing.

It had only been a couple of hours but the time out had done them all a world of good. The situation had become very stressful, and Douglas hoped that McAfee could bring things to some sort of a resolution quickly. It was beginning to wear on all of them but especially Dede, who needed to be back home with her Mother for sure but not until it was safe for her to return. The girls headed out into the back yard to grab some more sun and Douglas flipped open his laptop to get to work on the outline for his article on human trafficking and on Nash in particular. The fact that such a man was so close to the Governor's mansion was a scary reality, not that he hadn't seen and reported on corruption before. But there was a vast difference between taking a few kickbacks and selling children for sex. Conrad Nash was truly a scumbag, and it was going to be a real pleasure to bring him to his knees and see him off to prison. But first things first, to focus on his writing, and to sip this awesome coffee.

"They are nothing if not predictable," Dexter told McAfee. "They were both right there in the same bar that they always hang out in."

"Creatures of habit," McAfee mused. "I'm hoping that the idea of going back to prison for decades might get them talking. Maybe we can sell them on giving up Nash in exchange for a few years off. A chance to be back out before they are too feeble to enjoy it."

"I dunno. If they have half a brain between them they know damn well that any judge in Georgia is gonna put them away for a very long time. I wouldn't be surprised at forty years."

"Well they have it coming to them, that's for sure. But I'd personally be happy to see them roll on Nash and get twenty for themselves. He's the much bigger threat. Otherwise he's free to just move operations elsewhere and keep on destroying these kids."

"We're gonna split them up and lean on them hard. All we need is for one of them to break."

Joey Pastore and Rodney Jones were two street level punks who were most definitely followers, not leaders. They had been in and out of the system for years with arrests from Athens to Atlanta and even in Jacksonville. They were the type to sell their own girlfriends for fifty bucks, not to run large scale trafficking operations. They had a splattering of drug arrests, always relatively light weights, along with a couple of burglary raps and resisting without violence. They had never been arrested on gun charges, and were not known as enforcers by any stretch of the imagination. They were both uneducated, having not gone much further than the eight grade, and even in the city they still presented as rednecks.They had known one another since serving time in juvenile detention, and where one was the other was surely close by. It was entirely likely that neither one of them understood the magnitude of the crimes they had been recently committing, and so would be caught very much off-guard to hear that they were facing a possible life sentence once their prior records were considered.

Dexter and the other detectives decided to begin with Pastore, who seemed to be the weaker of the two when it came to interrogations. He sat stoic, clearly worried but not as much as he should be. Unlike Simmons he made full eye contact, was prison hardened, would not be intimidated by the prospect of doing a little time. But how about life?

"So Pastore...you're a four time loser. I see you sittin' there lookin' all tough. Ain't nobody gonna intimidate you. Right boy?" Dexter grinned. "Lemme just tell you how many years you're looking at….all of them."

Pastore smirked back at him. "All of what?"

"All of your years you dumb shit. All of 'em."

Pastore tried not to register any expression but this revelation caught him clearly off guard.

"What the hell are you talking about?"

"Oh wait wait wait," Dexter shook his head with exaggeration, mocking the man. "You thought this was gonna be like a burglary rap or a drug rap, right? No no no boy. This is human trafficking, sexual exploitation of possibly hundreds of minors, rape, conspiracy, solicitation, kidnapping, false imprisonment, numerous felony assault counts. It all adds up to nobody's ever gonna see your pathetic ass on the outside ever again."

McAfee watched from the other side of the glass, actually a little impressed. He liked Dexter. He was young but far from green. It was very clear that Pastore had no idea how much trouble he was in. The guy was just a low level hustler who somehow crossed paths with Conrad Nash or someone close to him. All they needed from this guy was a name. If he just gave up the name he might, maybe, have a chance at parole. Here's the thing that most people didn't get. A judge can do whatever the hell he or she wants to do. They can accept the deals that have been made or reject them. They can even force you into a jury trial that you didn't want. Discard your plea deal in order to send you up for life. It all depended on the judge and what you did. Does the judge maybe have a daughter? Then you're screwed. Do they not like your lawyer? Then you're screwed. Maybe they don't like the cop that arrested you? Maybe you catch a break. But one thing was for sure. It didn't matter worth a crap what a cop tells you in an interrogation room. Maybe some assistant district attorney offers you a deal. Great. Maybe.

Dexter had given Pastore a few moments to let it all sink in. He didn't look quite as cocky now.

"Look, Pastore, I'm talking to you and your dumb ass buddy Rodney Jones. One of you is gonna catch a break and one of you is going into the pit forever. I don't like either one of you dipshits so I don't really care which is which. Whoever talks to me first...then I put a good word in. That's that. You ever wanna touch a woman again? Sip a cold beer? Eat a steak or maybe some nice seafood? Then you better tell me what I need to know."

"You don't understand…" Pastore was visibly nervous now. "I can get killed."

"Give us the good stuff. All of it. Then maybe we can work out protection for you. Maybe you do your time really far away from here. We work that stuff out all the time. When we feel like it of course."

"I work for Smitty Black. He controls everything here in Athens."

Richter and Massey nodded.

"We know him," Massey told Dexter. "He did twelve for second degree murder and a couple shorter stretches for extortion and assault. He's muscle."

Dexter stood up in place to stretch his back. "Well, that much might get you some protection but not much of a deal. I hope you know the big man's name."

Pastore looked like a man on the edge of a cliff with a spear to his back.

"I never talked to him personally. I'm just a door guy."

"But you've seen him."

Pastore sighed. "Yes, I've seen him."

"And you know his name."

Pastore buried his face in his hands, staying quiet for a few moments.

"Conrad Nash. His name is Conrad Nash."

On the other side of the glass McAfee pulled his cell from his pocket and pushed a button.

"Yeah Douglas, start writing your article. We got this piece of crap."

Casey was trying her very best to look reassuring but she knew her palms must be as clammy as Dede's. The girls had gone out behind the cottage to sit at the picnic table and call Dede's Mama. Dede looked across the table at her, eyes already moist, and took a deep breath.

"Hey," Casey reached across and took her hand. "Whatever happens with this, we got you. Okay? Maybe it goes as it should, maybe. But we got you regardless."

Dede nodded and dialed the number. It rang a few times and seemed like maybe no one was home but then…

"Yeah what? Who's this?"

Dede's face registered panic. "Dennis" she barely whispered. Casey took the phone.

"Hi, Is Miss Clara in please?"

"Whos' asking?"

"This is Casey down at the nursing home. Just calling to see if she might be interested in a bit of double time."

"Shit, fine, hold on."

Casey put the phone on speaker and placed it on the table. After a moment Dede's Mama came on. "Hello?"

Dede took another breath. "Mama."

They could hear the emotion in her voice over the line. "Hold on just a sec."

Then after a moment. "Baby? Oh my God my sweetness."

Dede began to cry. "It's me Mama."

"Sweet Lord in heaven, where are you?"

"I'm with a friend, Mama. A few friends, and I'm safe."

"Girl, oh thank God. Where have you been?"

"I have something to tell you Mama. About why I ran."

"Whatever it is, baby. You know it's always you and me. Whatever it is, I love you okay?"

"Yes Mama."

"Oh lord, I'm so happy to hear your sweet voice."

"Mama…"

"Tell me, Dede."

"It was Dennis, Mama."

At first they didn't know if she had hung up. The line went dead quiet. Then…

"What did that piece of shit do?"

Dede began to sob now.

"Baby," her Mama cried on the other end.

"You had gone off to work, Mama, and I was alone."

All three of them were crying now. Dede clutching Casey's hand tightly.

"Please come home to me baby. Or I'll come to you, whatever you want. But he'll be out today. We can go to the police if you want...or just have some of your Daddy's old friends handle things."

Dede wiped her nose with her sleeve. "I can't come right now Mama. But real soon, okay? I have more to tell you and my friends are gonna bring me home."

Casey spoke up. "Hi Miss Clara, I'm Casey. Dede is safe with us, I promise, and we're fixin' to have her home real soon."

"Thank you, thank you. I'm so happy right now."

"Yes Ma'am."

Casey left Dede to speak with her Mother a little longer and went inside to talk to Douglas.

He looked up from his computer as she entered the room. "Are those happy tears I hope?"

"Yes. It went really well. I think maybe she had a suspicion but didn't know for sure till now."

Douglas nodded. "She's gonna have to make some hard decisions soon. It's harder now to press charges but still possible to try. Especially since she's a minor."

"They should move outta that town."

"Well, hard to do when you're broke. But who knows? Maybe some of Mac's new cop friends in Athens can give her Mama a lead on a new job."

"Yeah." Casey sat down beside Douglas and rested her head on his shoulder.

"I'm really lucky."

He kissed the top of her head. "Yeah kid. Me too."

"How the hell did that happen!" McAfee shouted at the detective on the other end of the line. He and Dexter were headed back to Savannah and had already made contact with the local ADA to begin work on warrants to arrest Conrad Nash and search his properties and office in Savannah. All the paperwork was being assembled along with transcripts of the interviews and witness statements from Dede, Carly and Loren A'mico. Once the packet was ready they would rush it over to Judge Raymond Claiborne who was waiting to sign the warrants. But there was now a major problem.

"I thought you had somebody on him!"

"Sorry McAfee," the detective answered through the car speakers. "We had a guy sitting on his house but he must have gone out the back. There's no sign of him anywhere now."

"You're telling me a high profile guy like Conrad Nash just walks out the door without anybody noticing? Trained cops! Detectives!"

"Get everybody out there," Dexter jumped in. "Everybody. This is the biggest case on the table right now. If he manages to get on a plane…"

"Get people on the damn airfields!" McAfee shouted again. "Public and private!"

"Trains and buses too," Dexter added.

Dexter had activated his car's emergency lights and siren as they flew back toward Savannah.

"I mean, he can just drive off," Dexter shook his head.

McAfee was pissed. "Sounds like that's exactly what he did."

"His own cars are still at his house. Somebody scooped him up."

"Get them on his personal staff. Let's get all their tag numbers and addresses. But hell, it could be a friend, a taxi, an uber."

"I know. Man, I shoulda stayed on him myself."

"You needed to be in Athens. You did outstanding work Dexter. And shit, are you gonna write tickets in the fire lane too? What the hell are all these other jokers doing?"

"I know, I know. Believe me, heads are gonna roll."

"They better find his ass."

"We will."

Douglas hung up the phone in disgust. "No," he answered Casey, who'd been waiting for an answer when McAfee had called.

"But it's just a little Christmas shopping."

"It's just too dangerous, kid."

"But we can drive over to Georgetown. Nobody's gonna be lookin' for her out there."

"Look," Douglas took Casey by the hand and led her out of earshot.

"Nash is in the wind. The locals lost him."

"What!"

"We need to stay as low as possible Casey. No witness, no case. They need her gone."

"Oh my God. How could this happen?"

"Don't know. But this is on a higher level than we're used to. This guy is very connected and very rich. He's not going down without a fight."

"Do you think someone tipped him off?"

"There's no doubt. Probably the brass hats in the police department. They love the guy. So for now, please, keep yourselves occupied in the cottage. No more outside at all. Okay?"

"Okay."

Casey walked back into the bedroom where Dede was watching funny youtube videos on her bed. "This dog can say hello," she laughed.

Casey smiled. It was good to see Dede just being a kid and enjoying herself.

"Hey, I'm thinking of calling my friends Emma and Sasha later on video chat. I wanna introduce you guys."

"Okay, cool."

"I need them to do me a favor and grab some Christmas gifts for me. Those bitches love to shop so they'll be cool with it."

Dede got quiet for a moment. "We never had much money for Christmas back home."

"Yeah, we never did either. We never even had a tree or sang a Christmas carol in my house when I was a kid."

"Gosh. My Mama would bake some cookies at least and give us candy that she bought with her food stamps. But we'd always sing and she'd read me a Christmas story."

Casey smiled. "That sounds real nice."

"It was. What y'all do for Christmas now?"

"Well," Casey sat down beside her on the bed. "Douglas thinks he's a good cook so I s'pose he'll butcher somethin."

Dede chuckled.

"Then I guess maybe we'll open a gift or two and maybe watch a good Christmas movie on tv."

"That sounds nice too."

"Yeah, it really does."

"What the hell do you mean you couldn't spare the officers?" McAfee was absolutely infuriated. He stared down a bored looking Captain in the Savannah PD's major crimes office. The man shrugged.

"Look, sorry. You are not a priority and, I might add, you're not even a goddamned cop anymore so stop thinking that you're gonna come in here barking orders!"

McAfee got up as close as possible without touching the smaller man. "Listen, you corrupt piece of shit. I know what this is and let me tell you, you don't want any part of what it's gonna buy you."

"Dexter," The Captain scoffed. "Get your boyfriend outta here before I cuff his ass up."

Dexter placed his hand on McAfee's arm but did not attempt to pull him away. After staring the Captain down for a moment McAfee shook his head. "Fine. Your ass can go down with him." He turned and walked out of the office and down the hallway to the main doors with Dexter close on his heels.

"We still have a few guys assigned," Dexter was saying.

"Yeah, well, I have a few of my own too. And I'll tell you what, that ol' boy is not makin' it out of Georgia no matter how many corrupt cops he has running interference for him."

"You want one of our cruisers to stay with the girl?"

"Hell no. We'll take care of Miss Dede on our own. Just have everybody you can checking on his closest associates and hopefully we'll catch a break. Also, if you could try and get his banking records maybe he'll show up somewhere to withdraw cash."

"Yup, you got it."

"Alright brother. I'll be out searching. You have my cell."

McAfee walked to his car and climbed in behind the wheel. He sat for a moment trying to think of what Conrad Nash's next move might be. The boy was high profile. He wasn't like some common criminal who could just blend in anywhere. With the APB out on him the Georgia news outlets were gonna smell a story and come running. Which was another thing. Douglas needed to go on and put out an initial story before anybody else did. After all, they were still in the news business and they are the ones that worked the investigation. He shot Douglas a text and received a quick reply... "Already on it." He thought for a moment and sent another text. "Hey Douglas, I could use Malone out in the field with me. Tell her be ready in fifteen and bring her laptop."

Douglas answered immediately. "She said she'll be ready."

McAfee couldn't help but grin to himself as he drove. Who woulda thought that the skinny little blonde tomboy that he'd booked for murder not too long ago would become one of his most effective investigative assets. He had to admit, but only to himself, that he was really proud of her. She'd been kicked around all her life but risen above it all, in large part thanks to Douglas, and was now a successful young woman of abundant talent. She was still a major league pain in the ass, but that was her age not her character. He'd been stuck on surveillance with her once for two hours that felt like fifteen. The kid talked about vampires and castles and books, movies, music, karate, and for half an hour about some dumb ass short story she'd read in class at the community college. She talked about Switzerland, for some damn reason that he couldn't remember, and about how men shouldn't be allowed to wear sweatpants in public. But he loved her. He couldn't lie. She and Douglas were the two realest people he knew, and they seemed to like having him around too.

He made his way down toward the river and cut up past the old cotton exchange, waiting a moment for a horse and buggy to slowly pull to the curb to scoop up some tourists with eighty bucks to blow on a half hour tour. Five minutes later he was back out of the historic area's commercial center and coming into a more residential neighborhood with cute little houses and rental cottages. He made a left and then a quick right onto Old Mill road where their temporary lodging was. He pulled into the dirt patch that was used as a driveway and decided to run in quick and hit the head. He climbed out and closed his door but suddenly felt the need to turn and look behind him. Decades on the job had sharpened his senses and something just felt...off. His eyes narrowed as he searched along the small yards and wooded patches across the shaded street, searching for whatever might be causing his unease. He couldn't shake the feeling of being watched.

Casey came out the front door of the cottage with her computer tucked under her arm and looked curiously out at McAfee. "We going?"

"Get back in the house," he responded without turning and she immediately did as instructed. Douglas, who had been working on his story, heard the exchange and jumped to his feet. "Grab Dede and lock yourselves in the bathroom. The hallway one with no windows. Now!"

Casey moved quickly to obey without question. She grabbed Dede from the bedroom and ran with her toward the bathroom, grabbing a kitchen knife from the butcher block holder as they passed by. Douglas stayed low and moved over to his briefcase, removing and cocking his Glock 17. He had no sooner done so when the first shot tore through the living room window.

"IN THE TUB! DOWN LOW!" he shouted to the girls.

Outside the sounds of a gun battle ensued. Douglas crawled over to the window and tried to peek out enough to spot where Mac was. The gunfire was continuing but from which direction he couldn't tell. He couldn't see the front of McAfee's car well enough from his vantage point but hoped that his friend was down safely behind it.

"MAC!" he shouted. No answer.

"MAC! YOU GOOD?" Still no reply.

He managed to slide the window up just a few inches and fired off ten of his seventeen rounds out toward the woods across the way, just hoping that's where the onslaught was coming from. He wanted whoever the attacker or attackers were to know that they were armed inside the cottage. He continually glanced back over his shoulder to make sure nobody was coming in the back door.

"CASEY?" he shouted.

"WE'RE OKAY!" she called back.

"STAY PUT!"

Another short burst of gunfire rang out and this time Douglas could clearly make out that half of them were being fired somewhere close to the cottage. Then there was the sound of tires screeching, another five or six gunshots...then silence. Douglas stayed down low by the window, glancing back and forth from front door to back, when he finally heard McAfee's voice. "Coming in the front!"

McAfee came in quickly, staying very low himself, and crouched down beside Douglas. "Where are the girls?"

"They're okay. In the tub."

McAfee peered out over the window sill.

"Are we clear?" Douglas asked.

"Not sure. I think so."

"I was calling out to you."

"Sorry. I tried to get around through the neighbors a bit and see if I could place their position."

"They must be Nash's guys."

"Yup, and they're cops."

Douglas looked startled. "Cops? You saw them?"

"No. I just know. Nobody else tracked us down that easy. We were all too careful. I'm thinking they followed me from the damn station."

"Even so, you got out of the car right away. I heard your door. How'd they get into position that quick?"

"Y'all didn't tell anyone where you were. The only one I told was..."

"Who?"

"Dexter."

"No. That doesn't make any sense. He got the guys to turn on Nash. Maybe they traced my cell?"

"Maybe. Yeah, maybe."

Douglas called out for Casey and Dede to come out but stay low. They came as far as the hallway then stopped, staying down on their knees. McAfee moved quickly to the back door and did a fast sweep of the back yard. He came back in immediately.

"Alright, listen. We're not taking any chances. I can hear sirens coming in the distance. Take the girls and go. Drive to Walmart, buy a burner phone and leave yours in your car. Call a cab and get about an hour out to another motel. You too, Malone, cell stays in the car at Walmart."

Casey nodded.

"Wait three hours Douglas. Then call me and tell me where you are. I'll follow the same routine."

"I'll go pack quick," Casey started moving toward their room.

"No, just go, now. I'll get it all. Go, go!"

Douglas grabbed his keys, computer and briefcase and headed out the door. He and McAfee stayed right beside the girls until they were in the car and down low in the back seat. Douglas sped away in the opposite direction of the sirens as McAfee made his way back inside. He surveyed the damage, quickly counting three shots that made their way inside the cottage without even looking very hard. The flat screen was hit, as was the microwave and a framed drawing of the old river ferry. He shook his head. "So much for our deposit."

Seconds later there were seven police cruisers and three black suv's in front of the cottage. Dexter was in the door first, gun drawn.

"All clear," McAfee told him. "Wish you were here fifteen minutes ago."

"What in the hell…"

McAfee made a split second decision to trust Dexter. "Cops."

Dexter didn't look as surprised as he should have. "You saw someone?"

"No."

Dexter looked outside as the Captain made his way toward the door. "Keep it with us."

McAfee nodded.

The Captain was clearly angry. "Hand over your weapon Mister McAfee."

McAfee complied, unholstering his glock and passing it to Dexter.

"You care to tell me why you were shooting up a nice residential street in my town?"

"I was ambushed. Getting out of my car."

"Who else is here?"

"Just me."

The Captain walked quickly through the cottage, spending a few moments to check and see if the closets and dressers still had clothing in them. He came back to face McAfee.

"Where are the others?"

"I have no idea. I barely had a chance to get in the door. There were multiple shooters."

"You see anybody?" Dexter asked him again in front of the Captain.

"No, I think the fire came from the woods across the way."

"Any vehicles?"

"An older model Chevy sedan sped off. Blue I think. I might have hit it once or twice."

"No others?"

"Don't know."

"Could you see how many guys were in the car?"

"No. They were too far off. At least two."

After a few more routine questions McAfee took a seat at the breakfast counter as a couple of detectives recovered the bullets lodged throughout the place. They even found one that he hadn't spotted, in the sofa throw pillow that he knew Douglas used to support his back as he worked. If he had still been sitting there…

"Your alleged witness is going to be under Savannah police protection from here on out," The Captain stated. "This is not up for discussion."

"I have ten of Atlanta's finest on their way out for her," McAfee lied.

"You heard what I said. This is not Atlanta."

"Well, Captain, you can fight it out with the Atlanta Commissioner if you choose. He'll just have to jump on the phone to the Governor and get it all sorted."

The Captain's eyes flashed nothing short of full hatred for a second, before the man simply turned and walked out.

Dexter walked over to him, pulling out another bar stool to sit down beside him.

"I think he likes you."

McAfee took a pack of gum from his pocket, offering a stick to Dexter as well who accepted. "I think he's trying really hard to get his hands on Dede."

"When will your boys be out here from Atlanta?"

"They should be close," he lied again with the same ease as before. She's gonna be under heavy cover from here on out."

While the drama continued to play out at the cottage, Douglas waited at the Wal-Mart electronics counter while they activated his twenty dollar phone. Casey and Dede had run quickly to grab some shorts and t-shirts for themselves, Douglas and Mac. They guessed underwear sizes as best they could for the men and grabbed a couple packs for themselves just in case McAfee got hung up. They also grabbed a case of water and assorted snacks, and met Douglas back at the counter just as he was ready to check out.

"We good?" he asked.

"Yeah," Casey answered. "For a couple days if need be."

"Okay, let's hit it."

They pushed their cart outside and waited for the cab to arrive that Douglas had called from his own cell before locking it back in his car. He had the cab drop them in the newer part of the city near a shopping mall, waited for twenty minutes, and then called for another from the burner phone. He asked the driver to bring them to the part of town with the most hotels and they were dropped off by a row of chain lodgings and family restaurants. He led the girls inside a hamburger place and they found a quiet booth near the back. After ordering three cheeseburgers with fries he placed a call to Sammy. She picked up immediately.

"Yeah?"

"It's me."

"God, Douglas. It sounds like all hell's breaking loose. Mac's been texting me."

"Yeah, this is my reach number for now."

"Alright. Tell me what you need."

Douglas looked out the window. "Two double rooms at the King's motor lodge in Savannah. Not in my name and paid in advance."

"Hold the line."

After nearly ten minutes Sammy came back on. "Done. Carl Chambers. Paid in advance by Be Best Plumbing, my brother-in-law's company. Better not to have it in the paper's name either."

"Good thinking."

"You sure you're all okay?"

"Shaken, but everyone's fine. I'm also sending you my initial story, check your email. Sorry about the poor editing, I was just starting on revisions when all hell broke loose."

"No worries, I'll clean it up."

"I'd get it out quick boss. On the web tonight and paper tomorrow."

"Absolutely. You sure you won't be safer back here at home?"

"I'm sure Nash has cronies there too. We'll stay put for now. At least till he's picked up by one of the honest cops."

"Damn, Douglas. This thing is huge."

"Run it boss, quick. Before the rest of the world jumps our story."

"Right. Bye."

"Bye."

The girls had already started in on their burgers, their appetites clearly unaffected by the near death experience of earlier.

"You girls both okay?" he asked anyway.

Casey nodded, putting her fist in front of her mouth as she chewed. "Yup. Pass the ketchup please."

He passed it to her. "Dede, you okay love?"

She smiled at him. "Yessir."

"Okay then, good talk." He hadn't realized how hungry he was until he took the first bite of his own burger. That explained the silence from across the booth. The poor things were half starved.

They ate in silence for a bit, enjoying the peacefulness of the meal after hours of chaos. Douglas checked his watch. Another twenty minutes and his story would be up online and distributed to the associated press. They in turn would circulate themselves 'as reported by Douglas Powell of the Atlanta daily.' Within an hour it would be all over the internet and breaking on the cable news. He grabbed the burner phone and punched in McAfee's number while he finished the last of his fries. McAfee answered on the third ring.

"Hey honey. Sorry I didn't have a chance to call you earlier."

Douglas smiled. "Well you owe me some flowers and candy."

"Everything okay at home?"

"King's motor lodge. The rooms are under Carl Chambers."

"Oh that's good. I bet you been playing with the baby all day."

"Everything okay there?"

"I'm fine, love. Same old. Just a little while longer for today then I'm going inside for a nap."

"Sammy's got the story. She'll have it out quick."

"That's good to hear. The other kids are all ok?"

"Everybody's fine."

"That's what grandbabies are for. So I'll talk to you later, okay?"

"Okay, love you," Douglas snickered.

"Oh yeah, me too."

The King's motor lodge wasn't half bad. They had connecting rooms on the second floor overlooking the restaurant they'd just left. Douglas had ordered another burger and fries to go so that McAfee would have it to warm in the microwave when he met up with them later. Casey and Dede emptied out the snacks and clothing they'd picked up at the store while Douglas searched for a news channel on the tv. He sat and watched the news coming out of Atlanta for about fifteen minutes, getting caught up on everything going on in other people's lives, before… "And this just breaking, The Atlanta Daily is reporting at this hour that State Representative Conrad Nash is wanted for questioning related to a sex trafficking investigation. A warrant has been issued out of the Savannah District court for his arrest. Authorities in Savannah were not immediately available for further comment."

"I bet they weren't," Douglas mumbled.

Casey sat down on the bed beside him. "This is crazy."

"It'll be international very soon."

"For real?"

"Yup. It's been a long day. You girls should really get some rest while you can."

"Okay, goodnight." Casey kissed his cheek and went through to her own room where Dede was already passed out on her bed.

Meanwhile, the Savannah PD had finally wrapped up their business in the cottage and had "left" McAfee on his own. The Captain had very reluctantly handed him back his weapon on his way out the door. McAfee had, of course, already spotted two unmarked cars on either end of the quiet street which were clearly waiting to follow him. But the ones who were clearly waiting to follow him were not the ones that actually would be. They knew he was a seasoned detective, so they planted two obvious tails while a third was somewhere close by waiting to jump in once he'd lost the others. They were smart, but not smart enough. He packed up all of their clothes and loaded all the bags into the rental car. Then, since he knew they were all set to follow him, he grabbed a can of soda from the fridge and plopped down on the sofa to make them wait. Just for fun.

McAfee woke an hour later, not at all surprised that he had nodded off. It had been a very long day and he wasn't as young as he used to be. He went into the bathroom to splash some water on his face, feeling refreshed from the short nap. Five minutes later he was pulling the car out and headed to Walmart. He waved to the cops at the end of the street as he passed, grinning from ear to ear as he thought about how they thought they could fool him. He didn't bother looking for the real tail car, he didn't need to. They could stay on his rental car all day and all night if they wished. He would be long gone and fast asleep by the time they figured out they'd been duped.

Traffic was relatively light by the time he'd left the cottage. He passed through neighborhoods with gorgeous Christmas light displays and headed out to new Savannah. The Walmart parking lot was still busy but he managed to find Douglas's car and was able to park right next to it. He left his cell in the car and casually walked into the store. The cops following him would assume he was making a quick stop for supplies, since all of their bags were in his car he was surely coming right back out. Except he wasn't. He walked in the front doors, straight to the back of the store, through the swinging doors that led to the storage bays, through an open door that a semi had just pulled away from, jumped down from the loading dock, and simply walked away.

They slept until nearly ten, the four of them exhausted from the chaos of the previous day. The girls had bought two packages of toaster tarts at Walmart so that became breakfast for the day. Douglas searched for more news on the television while McAfee fumbled with the coffee maker. Casey and Dede were taking turns brushing out each other's hair. Once the coffee was brewing Mac looked through the clothing the girls had purchased for him.

He frowned as he pulled a plastic package from the bag. "Seriously Malone? You got me briefs?"

He couldn't see her smirk from the other room but Douglas saw her and gave her a wink.

"God's sake girl."

"Well I don't know what kind of undies you wear," she called back.

He went to the doorway and squinted his eyes at her. "Do I look like a guy who wears panties?"

"Thanks for that image, old man. Just wear them. What's it gonna be, two days? Big baby."

He grunted something at her before heading into the bathroom for a shower.

The morning news confirmed the reports from the previous evening but nothing new. Douglas grabbed the burner cell from the night stand and called Sammy at the office. She was obviously waiting for his call and answered immediately.

"You guys okay?"

"Thanks to you. What's going on with the story?"

"Well everybody's picked it up of course. We knew that. Of course all the other news outlets are tying it to Casey. You know, Casey Malone involved in breaking sex trafficking case... and the team that broke the Casey Malone story is causing waves once again. We're getting requests for interviews that we can't keep up with."

"I worry about her name being out there again. I'm not sure how safe it is. You know how they like to hound her like the paparazzi."

"She wanted the gig, Douglas. And really, it wouldn't matter if she was involved or not. As long as you and Mac are they'll find a way to tie it to her. How's Dede doing?"

"Rattled but Casey seems to keep her as calm as possible. We'll all rest easier when Nash is picked up."

"She'll still be a witness. Whether he's in custody or not you'll need to be careful."

"Yeah but right now he's probably thinking she's the only witness. He may not know that the other guys turned on him."

"I'm worried about the ones that are still out there. We don't even know who they are."

"I know. I'm not expecting a tight little bow on this one. The truth is that we may never know who half of them are or even how far this reaches. It may cross state lines."

"Or even be international. I think we've barely scratched the surface here. There may still be cartel involvement."

"I'm working on another update story for you to run. We'll do one a day for as long as this plays out."

"You realize that may take years."

"Job security for me."

Sammy laughed. "Reach out later."

"Will do, boss."

McAfee came back out of the bathroom wearing his new 'Born for the beach' t-shirt that Casey had grabbed for him. He sat down on his bed and pulled his dress pants back on. "I'm not wearing shorts."

Douglas grinned. "The shirt fits you good."

McAfee looked down at it. "I like the beach.":

"There's nothing new on Nash."

"I'll call Dexter for an update but then we'll need to toss that phone and pick up another one somewhere."

"Yeah, sounds good."

"I was thinking," McAfee continued as he tied his shoes. "Once they scoop up Nash we could all run the kid back to Mississippi and make sure that Dennis guy is really gone."

"You ever hear of Bell, Mississippi?"

"Nope. I'm sure it's very glamorous."

"We were thinking maybe we might help her Mama find a better job somewhere else. Maybe here in Georgia."

"It might be better to use some of the paper's contacts and move them to Ohio or someplace. There's still gonna be a risk here."

"Yeah, true. Sammy just mentioned that."

Casey and Dede came into the room wearing their own new shirts and took seats on the little sofa.

"So what's the deal?" Casey asked.

"We're hunkered down right here until we hear that Nash is off the street at the very least.," Douglas answered. "Right now we don't even know for sure that anybody's looking for him."

"Which reminds me," McAfee jumped in. "I'll call one of my old buddies at the FBI and see if there's something here they can jump on."

"Okay. You're heading out?"

"Yeah. I'll call him and then Dexter and then get us another phone."

"Alright. I'll get to work on an update story for Sammy."

"Anything we can do?"Casey asked.

"I might need some help later," McAfee answered. "I'll get back with you in a couple hours."

The alley smelled like piss had been baking in the sun for days. McAfee tried to be careful where he stood as Dexter provided him with an update. It had cooled off a bit more, and both men wore their suit jackets as they talked. The alley, between the rear of a string of stores and the backyards of some garden apartments was a very good choice of meeting places if you didn't want to be spotted. Nobody was coming back here unless they absolutely had to. The dumpsters all needed to be emptied and Mac could make out the easily identifiable sound of rats.

"I meet my informants back here sometimes," Dexter read his mind. "Let's just say we've never been disturbed."

"You think Nash is still in Georgia?"

"Yup. And as of about an hour ago I think I know exactly where."

Dexter had McAfee's full attention. "Yeah? Where?"

"McCaysville."

"McCaysville? Way up in the mountains?"

"Yes. And right on the state line. He can jump across at any time if need be."

"Why there?"

"You asked me about people close to him. One of his aides mentioned property up there that Nash liked to visit here and there."

"That didn't come up in the property search."

"Cause it's not his. It's his father-in-laws. The old man is in his nineties and apparently never gets up there anymore. But Nash's wife loves the place. She spent a lot of her summers there as a kid."

McAfee was excited now. "Where's she?"

"Home here in town."

"You sure?"

"Verified myself."

"This is good work Dexter."

"I'm thinking we go up there on our own Mac. That way nobody can tip him off that we know about the place."

Two scenarios played out quickly in McAfee's brain. The first was that he and Dexter drove up to McCaysville, got the jump on Nash, and brought him in to face justice. The second, was they got up there, Nash wasn't there, and Dexter puts a bullet in the back of McAfee's head. Who knows, maybe the whole property story was a complete fabrication.

"Alright. Let's do it," McAfee agreed.

Dexter clapped his hands together once. "Perfect. I need to grab some equipment from the office. We can get you a vest too."

"You know what?" Mac raised his index finger as a thought struck him. Let's meet back here in an hour. Out in front though. I don't want a deep breath of this crap before I go for a car ride."

"Okay. An hour it is."

"Bring me a shotgun. Pistol grip."

Dexter nodded. "No problem. Anything else?"

"See you in an hour."

Dexter jumped in the car and headed out and McAfee walked about ten minutes to a discount cellular store and purchased two new burner phones before breaking the other one and throwing it in the trash. He made a quick stop inside a men's clothing store for a fresh dress shirt before carefully making his way back to the King's motor lodge. He calculated his moves in his head as he walked. His Glock was loaded and he had two additional magazines. He would give Douglas one of the cellphones and bring the other with him. He would have Malone verify the story about the wife's father owning the property in McCaysville. And he would call his kids to tell them he loved them, just in case. They were adults now and understood without having to ask. On the way back to meet up with Dexter he would contact his friend in the FBI and tell him everything they knew so far including their suspicions of law enforcement involvement. He would like nothing more at this point than to have the feds take control of the investigation. The problem was they needed cause to believe a federal crime had been committed.

Douglas wasn't at all happy with the new plan but recognized that there wasn't a whole lot they could do about it. Nash needed to be put away or Dede would not be safe. Maybe none of them would be. Plus if there was any chance at all of finding some of the other girls they needed to take the risk. As much as they wanted to see Nash go down, what they really wanted was to find all the other Dede's out there. McAfee was taking a huge personal risk though. If Nash was on the property up in McCaysville the chances were slim that he was alone. And when you factored in that they didn't one hundred percent trust Dexter…

"I could go with you," Douglas suggested. "At least you'd have one guy with you that you can trust."

"If things go bad you need to be able to get the girls someplace safe. Don't worry about me. I've had eyes in the back of my head for about thirty years now."

McAfee changed into his new shirt and re-holstered his weapon. He made his way into Casey's room where she was typing away.

"I found it," she announced without looking up. "I looked up his wife's family and found her father. Her dad was a big wig banker and it looks like he's friends with half the other big wigs in Savannah."

"The democrat half I'm guessing."

"Yeah. He was a city commissioner once."

"That's where Nash got a lot of his initial political support I'm guessing again."

"Anyway, he does own a twenty acre spread up in McCaysville. Looks pretty fancy, a six bedroom log deal with a barn."

"It's right on the state line?"

"You can walk across."

"Okay. Who's the law up there?"

Casey typed for a few seconds more. "County Sheriff."

"Where do I find him at?"

"Probably home taking a nap."

Dede laughed and McAfee couldn't help but laugh as well. "His office Malone?"

"About fifteen minutes from the property. Just a few deputies would be on, considering the department size."

"Good work. Thanks."

After a few more quiet words with Douglas the girls watched him leave. Casey noticed that Dede looked worried. "He's a big boy. A really big boy."

Dede smiled. "I don't want anybody to get hurt on account of me. Y'all have been so nice to me."

"Yeah. We kinda like you I guess."

Dede smiled again. "Do you think he's up there?"

"If he is, he has no idea how screwed he's gonna be in about four hours."

"Will it be safe once he's arrested?"

Douglas walked into the room and joined the conversation. "The guys that work for him work for money. When the pay stops they stop. They know very well that he's not getting out of this. So hurting you no longer benefits them once he's in custody. It would only bring them all more unwanted heat."

"I hope you're right."

"Yeah, so do we. You girls hungry?"

Casey perked up.

"Dumb question," he smiled. I think I can sneak us back something from across the street."

It was a long ride even utilizing the lights and siren for part of the way. They followed the interstate system, 16 to

75, took the Atlanta bypass, picking up 76 on the other side of the city and passing through Talking Rock, Ellijay and Blue Ridge before making their way into McCaysville. By some miracle it only took just over five hours, and they arrived at a quarter past six. It was already dark, which was a plus, but they didn't know the terrain, which was a minus. They were also tired from the ride and getting hungry, and decided it was best to eat, get a little sleep, and hit Nash early the next morning. Dexter pulled into a roadside diner just outside of town and they were grateful for the chicken and waffles and strong coffee.

The town was cute and mostly touristy these days, with shops all along the Toccoa river and tourist trains that ran between McCaysville and its sister city Copperhill Tennessee. The area was rich in mining history and there were museums and mine tours available for the throngs of tourists to explore when they escaped the crush of humanity that was now Atlanta. But the outskirts of town were still very rural and very clannish, not at all welcoming to the outsiders who felt entitled to hike or camp on private property or expect special treatment when stopping for gas or necessities at a small country grocery. They would be even less interested in answering the question of any big city cops, and even if Nash was sitting right beside them they would never say a word.

They found a cheap double room at a run down motel to formulate a plan of attack and hopefully catch a few hours of sleep. The property was twenty acres, and they would have no real idea exactly where the house and buildings were without doing some research at the tax assessor's office which they decided would be a bad idea. You simply had no way of knowing who knew who up here and it was too great a risk that Nash would get tipped off. McAfee remembered a story from about twenty years back. Some local boys from nearby in Morganton were running marijuana down from their Canadian source and distributing it throughout the region. The FBI had caught the case since they were crossing state lines and the word had been that they were heavily armed so the ATF got involved as well.

It wasn't easy building a case when the targets are damn near buried into some rural mountain property and folks would rather be boiled alive than talk to the cops. The feds had staked out the spot for weeks, but from so far back that they had no idea what the hell was going on inside the compound full of mobile homes, run down outbuildings and a house that had sat on the property since the turn of the century. Throw in the uncertain terrain and the heavy tree cover and it was a recipe for a raid disaster. And a disaster it turned out to be. The feds hit the place on a Sunday, early in the morning when there was barely a sound to be heard. Except for them. Their running feet, uniforms swishing through the waist high grass, and a little huffing and puffing gave them away long before the dogs had started barking.

The couple of ol' boys who were holed up there actually turned out to be twelve boys. Twelve very serious boys. They opened fire on the twenty agents assigned to the raid, taking out five of them before they even knew what was happening. Eleven more of them needed a ride to the emergency room, four of them in critical condition. The four who were left able bodied were driven back off the property, lucky to still be in one piece. It took a week for negotiators to talk the men out. Of course every scrap of evidence was gone by then, probably buried somewhere it would never be found. Cops? They asked. Damn y'all, we didn't know you were cops. Why didn't y'all say something? Or, ya know, call first? None of them served a single day in prison for the incident.

McAfee and Dexter had no possible way of knowing who was on the McCaysville property with Nash. Just like the challenges the feds faced twenty years ago, they were looking at a whole lot of scenarios. Some not so bad, some...well, they'd die. They could call on the locals for a warrant assist but who knew if they could be trusted? They were local boys, but also cops. And just like in Savannah, the local Sheriff might be looking forward to having a buddy in the Governor's mansion. In the end, they decided the risk was just too great to charge in without backup, and they made the phone call to arrange a meeting with the Sheriff at first light. They were mostly comfortable with it, managing at least to fall asleep right away.

Sheriff Gill Spencer was a local legend. He had a reputation that had every man who crossed his path calling him Sir. He wasn't as big as the stories would have you believe, standing just over five-ten and weighing in at about two hundred pounds. But he was built like a rock, with massive biceps protruding from beneath his short sleeve uniform shirt which though large, seemed small on him. His forearms could only be described as vascular, looking like he might have done a couple hundred heavy dumbbell curls before he came into the office. He shook hands firmly, but didn't say much until he, McAfee and Dexter had their cups of coffee in hand and took seats around his desk.

They weren't feds, so that helped, but the suspicion in the Sheriff's eyes didn't require any verbal confirmation. "So, y'all are workin' a case in my county? That right?"

"No Sir," Dexter answered. "We have a warrant out of Savannah in connection with a human trafficking case. We were hoping for your assistance with the arrest."

The Sheriff nodded, his face becoming suddenly concerned. "I been watching all that on tv. Y'all wanna pick up Conrad Nash. That so?"

"Afraid so, Sheriff."

"Mmm Hmm."

McAfee and Dexter stayed quiet for a moment as the Sheriff seemed to be thinking about his options. He made eye contact once again. "Well, his wife's Daddy has been awful good to our department. Donations for equipment, helping out injured deputies with their bills, that sort of thing."

McAfee nodded. "We know the family has an outstanding reputation, Sheriff. This is very hard for all of us in law enforcement."

"You got him dead to rights hey?"

"Afraid so Sheriff."

The Sheriff sighed. "Well y'all, duty's duty, right?"

"Yes Sir," Dexter nodded.

"We're sworn to uphold."

"Yes Sir."

"Alright. No time like the present. Let's go get after it."

Douglas listened to Casey and Dede giggling in the other room. They were watching some old eighties sitcom on the tv and poking fun at the hairstyles and outfits the actors were wearing. The sound of the two of them enjoying themselves made him smile. Both of them had been through far too much turmoil in their young lives. He was hoping as hard as he could that this would all be wrapped up within a day or two. Christmas was quickly approaching, and he wanted it to be a perfect one for Casey and for Dede to be back home safely with her Mama. Thank goodness for online shopping. It wasn't quite as personal, he'd find something great when they were back in the city. But at least he was able to order a few nice outfits that he thought Casey would like. It was always so hard to tell. She smiled and seemed overjoyed at anything he gave to her. So he tried his best to pay attention to things she'd stop to look at here and there, trying to stay tuned in to the ever changing personal style of a twenty year old.

Casey was suddenly in the doorway looking at him. "What you smiling about?"

"Just thinking about Christmas."

She smiled back at him. "It's gonna be awesome."

"What's on your wishlist?"

"Just to chill with you. I'm making some apple pie from scratch. I found a recipe online that looks amazing."

"I'll look forward to that."

"Will Mac be with his family?"

"I'm planning to ask. He and his wife are pretty much separated but living in the same house. His kids are grown and have their own."

Casey nodded. "Well, he should come to have Christmas dinner with us."

"You have a kind heart Casey."

"And I make good pie."

"We'll see."

Casey laughed. "Yeah you will."

He went back to his work on the Sunday feature that Sammy wanted from him. This was the big one, the naming of names and presentation of the case against Conrad Nash. He was hoping that Nash would name some of his associates in exchange for a few years off his sentence. But you could never tell with these things, and men like Nash, rich and powerful, could stretch these cases out for years. The question was how many years had he been involved in this illicit business. How many young lives had Conrad Nash and his cronies destroyed before they were finally caught?

Casey sat down on her bed and propped her back up against the headboard. Dede was engrossed in another show, some daytime talk show about catching people cheating. She never could understand why people would cheat. How easy was it to just end the relationship and walk away? She supposed that it probably came down to money most times, and that it was better to play around on the side than to give any of it up to the spouse you could no longer stand. But what about when they weren't even married? It just didn't make a whole lot of sense. Seemed like a whole load of stupidity to her. The more she thought about it though, the more she realized that she'd never been in any kind of deep relationship that went bad. They were all bad right from the start. Maybe the people that cheated had really loved the other person in the beginning and just didn't have the heart to break it to them now. Still, stupid.

It was funny to think about how the story of Casey Malone was, and still seemed to be, so intriguing to so many people. She couldn't find any differences between herself and the other people she interacted with every day. And yet most people didn't know their names and everybody seemed to know hers. She understood that the press loved murder. And based on how many true crime shows there were on tv lots of folks were very eager to consume the product that they put out. She was not the only person out there who was abused as a child. She wasn't even the only teen who'd had to resort to violence to free herself from abuse. And yet people wanted to meet her when they spotted her on the street. They wanted to ask her questions, take a selfie. But did they want to be her friend? Hell no. That crazy Casey Malone killed a guy.

She shook the thoughts from her head. The same ones she had nearly every day. Especially at times like these when she wasn't otherwise occupied. The truth was that she wanted people to like her but didn't care anymore if they didn't. She had a family now, and some very good friends. Which gave her an idea.

"Hey Dede, you wanna video chat with my friends?"

Dede looked up. "Okay, sure."

"I want y'all to get to know each other. They're both cool and they helped me through some really hard times. That way you can always reach out to one of us if you're feeling down or something you know?"

Dede smiled. "I'd like that."

"Come sit with me."

Dede climbed onto the bed next to Casey who dialed Emma from her laptop. It took just a few seconds for Emma's smiling face to appear on the screen. "Hey my peach. I was wondering where you'd gone off to?"

"Hey Em. You remember Dede."

"Of course. Hey girl."

Dede smiled. "Hi Emma."

"What y'all up to? And what's up with that hideous wallpaper behind you?"

Casey grinned. "Cheap motel."

"Oh lord. Should I even ask?"

"Probably not. Hold on, I'm gonna try to three way with Sasha."

"K."

After one failed try the screen divided and Sasha appeared. "Well, I thought y'all had forgotten about me."

"I just talked to you yesterday," Emma smirked.

"And what about you Miss Casey? You found some new fancy friends or something?"

"Just one new fancy friend. And I told Dede how cool it would be if we were all friends from here on out."

"Absolutely. We already are."

Dede smiled. "Thanks Sasha."

"Oh don't thank me girl. You have no idea what you're in for. We're all batshit crazy."

Douglas smiled again at the sound of the girls laughing in the other room. He checked his watch and saw that it was already past noon. He hadn't heard anything much from McAfee except for a quick text that the Sheriff was onboard to provide some backup. He didn't want to reach out in case they were involved in the operation at that very moment. It was risky all around for sure. They had no idea who they could trust on this one but they knew for certain that Nash had powerful friends and a whole lot of reach. The question was whether they would all stick with him or scramble to distance themselves for fear of any association in the sordid affair. But the raid would be dangerous regardless, and he was having trouble focusing on his work as he worried.

The property was manicured and meticulously kept, not at all what McAfee had been expecting. Of course, this was not the scene of the crime or some meth lab in the woods, this was the vacation home of a prominent Savannah businessman and politician. Of the twenty acres about half were wooded. Unfortunately the ten all around the main house were wide open and there was little to no cover at all save for a few scattered oak trees. If anyone was keeping watch they would be clear targets.

"Like I was sayin'," the Sheriff drawled, "I think we're better off driving the van straight on up to the front door."

"Yeah, I don't see another viable option," McAfee agreed.

"Alright then. Y'all boys go on back and get it on up right to the base of the driveway," he told two young deputies. They scurried off to carry out his order.

"Me and Dexter and McAfee here will go in the van with three more of you. I want you two to drive right on back across the lawn to cover the back door and you other boys follow behind us. Straight?"

The other deputies all nodded.

"Okay then. Let's go kick the hornet's nest."

From across the short distance the house looked calm and almost eerily quiet. That wasn't unusual in these circumstances. Tension had a way of making things seem much more sinister. But truth be told, McAfee didn't feel good about this one at all. People could be real dangerous when they had something to lose and Conrad Nash was facing losing his freedom, his career, his family, and pretty much anything else of value. Still, Nash himself was not the main worry. The man had employed some serious characters in an even more serious criminal enterprise. There was nothing worse than men who would sell other human beings for their own profit. You needed to be soulless and completely immoral to be in that business. If any of Nash's men were in that house with him they wouldn't go down without a fight. Then so be it. McAfee double checked his sidearm before loading the shells into the shotgun Dexter had brought along for him.

The equipment had all been checked, vests were on, and it was now or never. Sheriff Spencer looked first at Dexter then McAfee. The two men nodded. The Sheriff placed his cowboy hat back on his head, braced himself in the van and said simply..."Go."

The van made its way up the long curvy driveway, accelerating as it went. There was no immediate resistance. The deputy driving and the other riding shotgun were hyper alert for any sign of movement but saw nothing.

They were halfway to the door, with multiple patrol cars both behind them and flanking out to each side of the house. There was no way that someone keeping watch would not have spotted them by now. Three quarters of the way, nothing. They screeched to a stop in front of the door.

"Go! Go! Go! Go!" The Sheriff's men were tight. They moved in a nice clean formation, weapons raised and battering ram ready to go. They made it halfway up the steps before the shooting started. It came on so fast and with such ferocity that there was no time to react and fall back for cover. They were committed at this point, making entry whether they liked it or not. A huge young deputy that looked like he was probably a high school football star smashed the ram into the door, shattering the frame and sending splinters and hinges flying. The others moved forward without hesitation, led by Sheriff Gill Spencer, who was cool as a summer salad.

It was a cloudy day, and not particularly bright inside the main entry of the home. Several deputies had dropped to one knee with weapons pointed in all possible directions, searching for the source of the threat. They returned fire outward and upward, showering the upper landing with a storm of bullets, providing cover as their fellow officers moved further into the large house. McAfee moved quickly left, staying low and close to the wall as he cut over into a halfway and followed one of the more senior deputies into the barely lit space. The deputy came to a doorway and moved silently to one side as McAfee moved to the other. He nodded to McAfee who pushed through the doorway first, emerging into a formal dining room.

The room was darker than the hallway, shadows were everywhere. The two men swept the space quickly, their decades of combined experience guiding them and keeping their senses on full alert for the very slightest of movement. The sound of the gun battle raging in the front of the home was near deafening and they would need to watch one another's backs if they hoped to survive any sudden attack. They moved as though they'd been working together for years, the common standards of Georgia law enforcement training coming second nature as they moved. There was no closet in the room, only a display cabinet for some poor lady's good china. McAfee looked beneath the tablecloth, behind a buffet serving table...nothing. He waved the deputy back into the hallway.

They exited the room stealthily, McAfee keeping one eye out behind them as the deputy moved farther down the hallway. When he came to the second door they repeated the routine, with McAfee once again moving through the doorway first. This time it was an old time butler's pantry, with serving counters, a sink and refrigerator. But no threats. They moved on. The third door led to a larger space which looked like a sitting room. There were two additional doors in the room, perhaps closets, maybe exits back to the main kitchen area or a rear hallway. They cleared the room first, checking carefully behind sofas and easy chairs before taking up positions on each side of the first door. The door opened toward them, and McAfee pulled it quickly as the deputy quickly checked. Just a closet.

The rear door was the more concerning, being far more likely an exit to another space than an additional closet. The two men took their positions again on either side of the door. McAfee aimed his weapon toward the door as the deputy opened it and quickly looked inside. "Dark," he whispered.

McAfee pulled the burner cell phone from his pocket and switched on the flashlight before sliding it a few feet into the room. The deputy looked quickly inside once more and motioned that they would proceed. They moved slowly and cautiously, McAfee sliding the lighted phone with his foot, a few feet at a time.

The room was mostly empty, furnished only with a small desk and chair. There was a computer monitor on top of the desk with the dim power light slowly blinking. McAfee found the mouse and moved it slightly to bring the screen back up. Images appeared of the other rooms in the house. The firefight was continuing and had moved back into other areas including the vast kitchen. Several deputies were on the floor but the images were too grainy to see how badly they were hurt. Beside the computer was a set of keys, and directly before them another door.

McAfee and the deputy took positions once again on either side of the door, trying first to see if it might already be unlocked. It was not. McAfee gently tried each of the keys, reaching across to do so so that his body was shielded if anyone should begin firing through the door. He had tried three of the keys when he finally found the one that worked and unlocked the door. The two men took a deep breath before opening it up. They stayed perfectly silent and motionless for a few moments, straining to hear any sound over the gunfire raging throughout the large home. McAfee slid his cell phone once more through the doorway, illuminating a landing at the top of a deep staircase. He popped his head in and out quickly to search for any threat before moving forward and making his way down the steps. The Deputy grabbed McAfee's phone before following a few feet behind.

There was a bottom landing that turned to the left but it was impossible to see even a few feet ahead. The deputy tapped McAfee's shoulder and placed the lighted phone back on the floor, sliding it into the room about six feet. They could see the space was large, but couldn't make out very much detail beyond that. They could hear the violent sounds from up above them but nothing from the large basement. The deputy pulled his flashlight from its holster and swept the beam quickly around the room. Tarps covered what they assumed was old furniture, a couple of barrels and crates, a broken ping pong table. They moved forward toward the covered furniture, sweeping wide and fast with weapons pointed to see what lay behind. More than a dozen young girls, clutching to one another in fear, looked up at them with terrified eyes.

McAfee knelt down beside the girls and spoke softly to them. "Everything's okay girls, we're the police. This deputy is going to stay here with you and keep you safe until this is all over, okay?"

The girls nodded silently and McAfee stood back up. He looked at the deputy who simply nodded. He nodded back before making his way out of the basement and back up the staircase. The higher he climbed the closer the shots sounded. The fight must have found its way down the hallway that the two of them had walked earlier. He reached the top and peered out into the small room, the computer monitor still providing enough light to see that the space was empty. He moved back through and out to the hallway, pausing to determine which direction the shots were coming from. But they were all around, left, right and above.

He made the decision to head out to his left, back out toward the main entry of the home. He was hyper alert, glancing back quickly behind him every few feet. When he finally reached the foyer it was empty. The Sheriff and his men must have pushed the attackers back into the heart of the home. He moved quickly back, passing beneath the massive double staircase and toward what he assumed would be the main living room. He was correct. As he made his way the space opened up to a great room, with comfortable furniture before him and an open kitchen to the left. The gunfire had subsided a bit, with a few random shots here and there but not the rapid fire of earlier. He spotted Sheriff Spencer crouched down low behind a sofa table and the Sheriff motioned for him to stay put. He got down low and waited.

"We got seven. We think there's only two more and they might be out of ammo," the Sheriff called over quietly.

"We've got about fifteen girls in the basement," he answered.

The Sheriff looked stunned. "Dear lord."

After just a few more moments of waiting the Sheriff spoke again. "You ready?"

"Yeah," McAfee answered. "Let's get this done."

He took the lead, with the Sheriff and six deputies close behind, first clearing the kitchen where a man lay dead behind the counter and then moving back into the hallway which led to the bedrooms. Several men lay dead in the hallway, and two more in the first bedroom they checked. Next was a hallway bathroom where another man was slumped over the tub. McAfee checked quickly for a pulse but found none. They continued forward, with no resistance and no more gunshots, eventually reaching the master bedroom. The men spread out quickly, checking behind furniture and under the bed before focusing on the closed closet door.

The Sheriff and his deputies aimed their weapons at the closet as McAfee moved to one side of it, preparing to pull open one of the double doors. A deputy moved to the other side to do the same. McAfee raised three fingers, counting down before he and the deputy threw open the doors to the massive closet which must have been fifteen feet deep. McAfee and the Sheriff moved forward, using their shotguns to move clothing to the side as they searched for any other threats. They spotted a chest of drawers toward the rear of the space, out several feet from the wall which seemed odd. They moved back cautiously before swinging wide and aiming their weapons behind the old dresser...at the cowering face of Conrad Nash.

Week Four

Bell Mississippi was everything Dede had said it was, which wasn't much at all. Casey had seen her share of impoverished neighborhoods growing up in rural Georgia but nothing like this. Bell seemed to be a town forgotten by time, overgrown by nature, and void of any hope for a future. The faces of the residents were sullen and tired, left exhausted by the daily grind of survival and nothing more. The few businesses in town were housed in old buildings that had seen their best days fifty years earlier, needing renovation at this point more than repair. Signs were faded, streetlamps broken, roads crumbling. People who could afford to had left years ago, moving out to Natchez or even up to Jackson where there was more job opportunity.

They passed by an old white church with boarded windows, a chain and padlock across the front doors. Casey shook her head at the misery of the place.

"The church closed up about six years back," Dede said, responding to Casey's non-verbal reaction.

"It all seems...harsh," Casey answered.

"It's funny. I'm not sure I realized just how bad it is until just now when we came back into town. I never had nothing to compare it to."

"Location is everything with these small towns," Douglas said from behind the wheel. "You're just not close enough to any metropolitan area or major highway to support much business."

"Most folks have small farms and such," Dede sighed. My Daddy used to make his living doing work here and there for some of them. There was just never enough to be able to break free of it. We were lucky sometimes to still have a roof."

McAfee had remained silent in the passenger seat as they made their way through town. When he finally spoke he sounded determined. "Yeah, we gotta get y'all up outta this shithole."

The others had to smile. McAfee was not known for his subtlety. "I mean, your Mama sounds like she's wanting to work so all you need is a fighting chance someplace."

"Yessir," Dede answered.

"Y'all have family here or anything keeping you?"

"No Sir. And we could pack up anything that matters in a couple of suitcases."

McAfee looked at Douglas who shrugged. "What're you thinking?"

"Well Atlanta's obviously a bad idea for Dede. Maybe, I dunno, Baton Rouge?"

Douglas nodded. "Someplace with enough of a hospitality industry to support full time work."

"Exactly. Maybe Sammy has some contacts?"

"I'll make the call."

They pulled up onto the front lawn of the small cottage as Dede instructed. There was no driveway and no lawn to speak of, just patches of high weeds and some gravel. Casey reached over and took Dede's hand. "You okay?"

Dede nodded silently.

"Maybe I should go in first. Make sure Dennis is gone and that you'll be safe."

"I'll go with you," Douglas answered. "I'd like a few words myself."

"Alright," McAfee looked out the window around the property. "Dede and I will wait on y'all."

Dede's Mother came to the door just as Casey and Douglas were about to knock. She looked as nervous as Dede.

"Oh my goodness. Is she here?"

Casey offered her hand. "Hi Miss Clara, I'm Casey. We talked on the phone."

Clara offered a little bit of a smile. "Of course, Hi Casey."

"Dede's here, but Douglas and I would like to come in and talk with you for a minute first if that's okay?"

Douglas nodded politely to her and she stepped back from the battered screen door. "Of course. Y'all please come in."

The inside of the small home was pretty much as expected. Old, but clean. The furniture was from the seventies, most likely by way of a thrift shop or church donation, with dark brown flower patterns and wooden arms. The floors creaked a bit, a few of the boards seeming as if they might be ready to give way. Clara motioned for them to sit and they did.

"Is Dennis gone?" Casey asked her.

Clara nodded. "Yes, for good."

"He raped your daughter."

Casey's directness caught even Douglas off guard for a moment but he was not surprised and understood her approach. Clara immediately began to cry.

"I'm sorry for the things you've suffered," Casey continued, "but this is not about you. You're the Mama, she's the child."

Clara wiped her eyes with a handkerchief and nodded. "I know. I thought...well, after my husband died I knew we needed to do something. We needed to keep from being homeless."

"A shelter would've been better. This will be with your daughter forever. And it didn't stop with what happened here."

Clara shook a little and wiped her cheek. "Was it very bad?" she nearly whispered.

"Yes."

Douglas stood up as they gave her a moment to compose herself. "May I look around the house?"

"Yes, of course. I promise he's gone."

"We need to see for ourselves."

Clara began to sob a little again. "How could this have happened? I always took care of her. Always."

He moved away down the hallway and Casey stayed with the broken woman.

"Are you willing to leave this place with Dede so y'all can have a better life?"

"We have no place to go. You think I haven't wanted that?"

"If we can find a way to help, will you go with it?"

"Yes."

"Right now, today?"

"Anything."

Casey got up and went to the door, motioning to McAfee that it was okay for Dede to come in. He climbed out of the car and opened the rear door for Dede. Clara came outside as she climbed out of the car and they ran to one another. The two clutched each other tightly and wept as Casey and McAfee looked on. After a moment Douglas came back out and joined them.

"You think we can get them out of here today?" Casey asked him.

"I'm gonna call Sammy. The place is barely livable. You can tell she does her best to keep things clean but it's just not safe. I'm worried about an electrical fire or something."

Casey sighed. "Seems like the people who need the most help are never the ones who get it."

"Yeah, I know. Throwing a few bucks worth of food stamps at folks like these doesn't fix anything."

"This is what I want for Christmas," Casey answered as McAfee walked over and joined them. "I wanna help them get what they need. I don't need anything."

Douglas smiled and hugged her to his side. "You have a very good heart kid."

"I can chip in," McAfee offered.

"Me too," Douglas replied. "Let's change some lives for Christmas this year."

With a few phone calls to Sammy and a couple other contacts, a newspaper editor down in Baton Rouge was able to line up a custodial job at the hospital where her husband worked. The Atlanta Daily offered the first few months rent and security deposit for the mother and daughter to find a nice place close to work and school. Douglas, McAfee and Casey decided that they would run them down and get them settled in before heading back to Atlanta to celebrate Christmas at home. They rented a van and packed up the things that were important to the two and headed down the road. The ride was only an hour and a half and the kind family who had arranged for the job also lined up a few furnished apartments for Dede and her Mama to choose from. They chose one close by to a cute little neighborhood park. It was small, two bedrooms that were far from generous and a galley kitchen, but they fell in love immediately.

Douglas and Mac assumed the duty of unloading and returning the van while Casey headed out with Dede and Clara for a Christmas shopping trip. Everyone involved, from the local paper to the new landlords were more than kind, they were Christmas angels. Casey couldn't help but feel an overpowering sense of holiday magic. It was as if they had transported into one of those heartwarming made for tv movies. She, Douglas and Mac were all kicking in five hundred dollars each for clothes, a Christmas tree, and a few nice gifts. Sammy had added another five from herself and armed with the two grand, the three women entered the mall. Clara and Dedw walked hand in hand with unfading smiles on their faces.

"It's good to see you two so happy," she told them.

"I am so grateful for you and the guys," Clara answered. "Thank you so much."

"It's our pleasure. This is a real chance for you two to build different lives. I mean, you can be whoever you want to be here."

"I'm fixin' to see if there's a GED program here," Dede answered. "I think that would be more comfortable than going back to high school."

"My college offers a high school completion program. Maybe they have something like that here. Especially if you're thinking of going on to college yourself."

The three walked and talked for a while, snooping around some shops before finding a budget friendly women's clothing store and beginning some serious searching. Dede told her mother some of what she'd endured since leaving home, perhaps finding it easier to be doing something as she described the ordeal rather than just sitting face to face. Her mother listened quietly, now and then reaching over to place a supportive hand on her daughter's back. The exchange made Casey comfortable with Clara's role moving forward, and convinced her that when Dede said her Mama didn't know about what Dennis had done she was telling the truth. She had feared that maybe she was just trying to shelter her Mom from any possible legal charge. She'd done that herself for years when she was growing up. There were never any obvious black eyes or burns, more bruising on her arms from when her daddy would grab her in a drunken rage.

Thinking of her Mama suddenly made her sad. Casey had always believed that her Mama was a victim of sorts too, though more so a victim of poverty and circumstance than abuse. But there had been a few good days. Times when her Mama would play with her for just a few minutes in the yard or tell Casey how pretty she was as she brushed her long blonde hair. She was probably a little drunk at those times but still, as a kid she hoped for those moments as rare as they were. It made her wonder where her Mama was now. She hoped that she wasn't back with her Daddy but sometimes people just couldn't help but do themselves harm over and over again. Casey simply refused to be one of those people, which is why she doubted she'd ever actually see her Mama again.

While the women shopped, Douglas and McAfee dropped off the rental van before driving back to Clara and Ded's new apartment and hopping on a video conference call with Dexter.

"You boys all good?" he asked them

"Yeah we're fine," McAfee answered. "How's the deputy doing?"

During the raid on the McCaysville property three deputies had suffered gunshot wounds. Unfortunately one had died at the scene from his injuries and the second was treated and released for a shot to his left leg. The third had undergone surgery to remove bullets from his shoulder and lower back. The latter had fortunately missed his spine.

"Serious but stable. The Sheriff says things look good for him."

"That's great news," Douglas said with relief. "I feel horrible for deputy Kelsey's family. We'd like to help with some fundraising for his funeral and to help his family out."

"Yeah, we'll pass the hat here in Savannah as well. So things are looking good for them in Louisiana?"

"Yeah," McAfee answered. "She's got a job lined up and this place is a huge improvement over what they had. Casey's got them out picking up clothes and stuff."

"Good to hear."

"What's up with the case?"

"Well Nash lawyer'd up just like we knew he would. I think we're gonna have to just accept the fact that there's gonna be more than a few loose ends on this one."

"Damn," McAfee groaned. "I was hoping we'd get some more names."

"Don't look like it brother. And I bet you this case crawls on through the courts."

"What's the prosecutor saying?" Douglas asked.

"She's a tough one. Debbie Silverstein. She's a hardcore republican, hated Nash's guts before she knew he was a child trafficker."

"So we know she won't be likely to drop the ball. How about Athens and Atlanta?"

"So the two boys we got in Athens might end up being all we get. Unless somewhere down the line Nash starts blabbering to save himself. We've got nothing in Atlanta except for your girl giving us this Clem guy's name. Atlanta says they'll pick his ass up today if we want but that since she admits to being a runaway he's likely gonna do a year and be back out."

"Yeah, let's hold off on ol' Clem," McAfee answered. "I have some plans for that boy."

Ten o'clock came around quickly. They'd helped cut tags off of new clothes and hung them in the closets, put up a couple of curtains, washed and put away new dishes and a pot set from Walmart. They went together to a Christmas tree lot and bought a nice Douglas fir with it's own reusable plastic stand. They went grocery shopping and stocked the fridge and small pantry. They felt completely confident by the time they left that Dede and her Mama would have a nice holiday and many opportunities for a much better life. They had an eight hour drive ahead of them, possibly less if traffic cooperated. They'd decided to take two hour shifts driving so they could catch a little shut eye. McAfee was in the back seat snoring before they'd even hit the highway. Casey yawned and turned to Douglas. "You sure you're okay driving?"

"Yeah, I'm good, baby. You should get a little sleep."

"Tomorrow's Christmas eve."

He smiled. "I made a call to Rolando. He put a nice six footer aside for us on the tree lot with a sold sign on it."

She smiled back at him. "It's gonna be hectic. We need to get the tree, pick up the groceries, and I'd still like to do a little bit of Christmas shopping."

"Way ahead of you. I did a full grocery order online and had it all delivered. Mrs. Webber from next door let them in and she very kindly put all the refrigerated stuff away."

Casey was beaming. "Are you serious? You got the turkey? And the cranberry? What about some pie or something?"

"Dutch apple and pecan. You know it."

They pulled onto the ramp for Interstate twelve, which would take them straight to sixty-five and right on up to Atlanta.

"Rolando's son will deliver the tree for us by the way. He said just give the boy a tip which I will be very happy to do. We can get the turkey on as soon as we get home, decorate the tree, and probably even catch a few hours sleep before we need to start cooking everything else. You think maybe you can do your shopping at the mall in an hour or so? Cause I can drop you there first, run home for the tree and get the turkey on, and then pick you up. Mac said his wife and the kids went to his daughter in-laws so he's just gonna crash on the couch at our place."

He found Casey's silence to be very unusual for her and glanced over quickly to see her sound asleep. He smiled, grabbed her hoodie from beside her on the seat and draped it over her. McAfee continued to snore in the back.

"Well, I guess I'm on my own for a bit." He turned on some soft jazz very low and settled in for the ride.

Just shy of six in the morning they made it home to the condo. McAfee had taken over the driving when they'd reached sixty-five and he drove the rest of the way back, leaving Casey to rest peacefully. He figured she'd be cooking as he napped later so let the kid get her beauty sleep. It was too early to have the tree delivered or start the bird so they agreed on sleeping till nine and then getting on with the Christmas cheer. But none of them rested very well. Unlike most of their cases this one simply was not fully resolved. Somewhere out there the other men who'd been involved in this trafficking ring were preparing to jump right back into it. That is if they'd ever stopped to begin with. And was Conrad Nash the big fish or just some guy that the cartel or east coast organized crime used to handle their local business?

Douglas tossed and turned for a bit before deciding to put on some coffee and maybe have a bagel. He'd managed to sleep a couple of hours in the car anyway and truth be told he really didn't feel all that bad. When he walked out quietly into the living room, so as to not disturb McAfee, he found the man already sitting up and checking emails on his phone.

"Can't sleep?" he asked him.

"Nah. You know how it is. I don't like loose ends."

"You're a pro, brother. Details matter."

"Yeah. Dede had mentioned rotating guards in Athens but we only managed to get two of the fuckers. I want them all."

"Me too."

"And we haven't even started here yet. You know damn well that the condo she was at was not their only place in the city."

"Coffee? Pancakes maybe?"

"Yeah, sounds good."

The two men went over the details that they did know while the coffee brewed. After a few moments the aroma brought Casey out from her room.

"It's not nine yet."

"We couldn't sleep," Douglas hugged her around her shoulders.

"Me either. I actually slept okay in the car."

"You snore like a bear," McAfee smirked.

"No old man. That's you. I thought the engine was maybe causing problems but it was just the sounds coming out of your mouth."

The men laughed as Douglas mixed some more pancake batter and began pouring spoonfuls onto the hot skillet.

"Sammy texted that she and Dan will come by for a drink and some dessert later."

"Sounds like a party," Casey smiled. "I need to pull out your Christmas albums."

"Nothing like the vinyl," Douglas agreed. "Especially those oldies."

They stuffed themselves with pancakes before stuffing the turkey and getting it into the oven. Casey checked to make sure they had everything else they needed and as usual Douglas had thought of every detail. The yams, fresh veggies, cranberry sauce and some nice soft dinner rolls were all there. And since their local market had its own bakery the pies looked and smelled amazing.

"Emma and Sasha gonna make it by?" Douglas asked her.

"They wanna stop by so we can exchange our little gifts before they head on home to Concord. I'm glad I get to see them for a little while anyway. We had planned to do a shopping day last week but taking care of Dede was much more important."

"It's nice that they've been reaching out to her. She can use all the friends she can get."

"Yeah and hopefully she'll be able to jump right back into school and meet some nice people there too."

"Tell them we have a slice of pie with their names on it."

"Will do. Wait...Cool whip?"

"Got it."

She smiled and kissed his cheek.

The three of them relaxed in the living room and sipped their coffee. It was still too early to arrange for the tree delivery or for Casey to head out to the mall.

"I'll tag along if you don't mind," Mac told her. "I could use a few things too."

"The more the merrier."

"Hey, Douglas took her hand. "I've got an early Christmas gift for you."

"Oh yeah? Now?"

"Yup, come here a minute. You too Mac, come check this out."

They got up and waited as Douglas opened the blinds on the sliding door out to the balcony. Casey spotted it before he had even slid the doors open.

"Oh my word, Douglas. You got the porch swing."

"Yes Ma'am. Had it installed while we were away. You like it?"

She sat down and kicked her feet a little.

"It's just like the one in Savannah. I love it!"

"He sat down beside her and patted her knee.

"This is just like the one we enjoyed at the bed and breakfast each evening, Mac. Casey had suggested we put one out here."

"Sounds like a nice memory for you two. It looks great."

Mac slumped down into one of the patio chairs and the three sat quietly sipping their coffee and just slightly swinging forward and back.

"When I was a boy," Mac smiled, "my Nanna had a swing out in the back yard under a pergola and she'd sit out there and do her knitting while we ran around with a ball in the yard. I can still remember her so vividly and the smell of her banana muffins coming through the kitchen window screen. She never checked the time or anything. Said she could tell by the smell when they were ready."

"She probably knew that when she started to smell them that it was a certain amount of time till they'd be done," Casey answered as she stared off into the morning sky.

"Somethin' like that I guess."

"Did y'all celebrate Christmas?" she asked.

McAfee sighed a little. "I don't know that you'd call it celebrating. It all depended on whether my Dad was on duty or not. But we had one of those artificial trees and always had a couple gifts to open so I suppose we were better off than most. My Mama always said one thing we wanted, one we needed and one to learn from. So maybe we'd get a toy, some socks and maybe a book."

Casey smiled. "I would've loved that."

"But if my Dad was around he'd be drunk and mean and so we'd stay as quiet as possible in our rooms."

Casey was loving the swing and more importantly the meaning behind the gift. She wrapped her arm around her new Dad's and smiled. "Okay, best and worst game."

"What's that?" Douglas asked.

"We tell each other about our best and worst Christmas. It has to be from before we knew each other. All three of us."

McAfee grunted. "Pass."

"No, come on," she prodded. "It's a bonding thing."

"I think we're pretty bound already. And you two are legally family now."

"You're family too," she insisted. "And you have to do it. Who wants to go first?"

Douglas shrugged. "I'll do it."

Casey squeezed his arm. "Good or bad first?"

"I'll do good first. But are you sure you wanna do this kid?"

"Yeah. It's important."

Douglas went inside first and carried the pot of coffee out to the porch, topping off each of their cups before setting it down on a dish towel so it wouldn't burn the wicker table. He glanced first at Casey then at Mac who just shrugged as if they had no power over this twenty year old girl who they both knew was going to get her way.

"Okay, so good first. I was about ten years old…"

It was Christmas eve 1970. Douglas, his brother and sister had been waiting all day for their Dad to get off from work so that the Christmas festivities could commence. His Mama had been in the kitchen all day long, baking the ham and lightly coating her famous sweet rolls with butter and honey just so, with the result being a heavenly experience that they'd look forward to each holiday season. After Christmas eve dinner they would light the tree which they'd already decorated earlier in the week, and they would all hold hands as his Dad said a prayer and asked the Lord to continue to bless their family in the new year. Then would come Mama's cherry pie and a generous dollop of hand whipped cream, never store bought, along with a nice glass of milk to make sure their bellies were completely full so they'd sleep like babies and not scare Santa away.

Their Dad had come home right on time and dinner was as amazing as ever. He told them all that he'd received not only a Christmas bonus but a perfect attendance bonus as well and that maybe come the springtime they could look into an above ground pool. They were all near giddy with the excitement and chattered on and on about how much fun the pool would be for the whole neighborhood.

"Y'all best finish up those greens if you're wanting to open your gift tonight," their Dad warned. A clean plate earns you one Christmas eve gift. Y'all know the rules of the game."

They'd scrambled to shovel down the bitter greens and grinned at their Mama as they did so, making their Dad chuckle just a bit as they tried to smile and compliment her on the dish that he knew very well they hated. Fortunately the cherry pie and cream came right after and erased the awful taste from their mouths. They'd cleared the dishes and washed, not arguing or shoving or talking smack to one another as was the norm at this time of the evening. They were the picture of lovely and obedient children and their Dad seemed amused by every moment of their over the top courtesy and kindness. Can I get you your slippers Mama? Would you like for me to take the trash out Daddy? He just laughed and shook his head at them. "Alright clowns. Y'all come set around the tree and Mama will bring you each one gift. Then it's off to bed without a fuss. Y'all hear? They all agreed quickly and took their seats to wait.

The gifts were all big. Daddy went to fetch them from the closet since they'd be heavy for Mama on her own. He set them down beside their Mama who'd joined them on the floor and she passed one to each of them. His brother was thrilled when he tore open the paper and saw his brand new boom box. "Not too loud in the house," Mama had warned with her pointed finger. He hugged her and promised and began to take the giant radio with dual cassette player out of the box to play with the many dials and buttons. His sister had nearly broken into tears of happiness when she saw her new sewing machine. She wanted so badly to be a famous fashion designer and this wasn't even a kid's machine but an actual grown up model. "I'm gonna teach you to measure out patterns and hem seams," their Mama said when she received her daughter's hug.

Douglas was always happy to watch everyone else open their gifts so he waited for his moment and enjoyed seeing everyone else so happy. His Mama turned her attention to him and winked. "Go on now baby. Let's see what you got in there."

He quickly removed the paper and could not control his excitement or emotions. It was a typewriter. And not one of the manual ones either...this one was fully electric. It said on the box that two extra ribbons were even included. He had never experienced happy tears before but a couple escaped him now. "Aww now," his Mama said as she pulled him into her for a giant hug. "My little writer is gonna be a big shot one of these days. I'm gonna walk into a bookstore or pass a magazine stand and see your name right there in big letters. My famous boy, the writer."

They'd all hugged their parents tightly before heading off to pretend they were asleep, thinking of all the fun ways they would use these amazing gifts starting the very next day. Douglas was old enough now to understand how much those gifts all cost and the sacrifice and hard work that went into giving them things that went beyond their needs and were simply to make them happy. He decided right there and then that he wasn't ever gonna argue or fuss anymore when Mama or Daddy asked him to do something. He was going to show them the respect and appreciation that they deserved and be the best son that he could be. And though he fell a whole lot short of perfect over the years he'd mostly kept that promise. And even though they were gone now their kindness and strength lived on through him and he had no regrets to live with over the way he'd treated them. And the typewriter...still on display in the living room. A prized possession.

McAfee offered Douglas one of his rare smiles. "So, your Mama knew way back then that one day you'd be writing about organized crime bosses and investigating sex traffickers."

Douglas laughed. "No. I think she had something in mind like maybe writing the great American novel. I don't think seeing me mess with powerful politicians would make her very happy. But she knew I loved to write. Back then I'd make up short stories and use that typewriter to build up my little portfolio."

"You still have some of your stories?" Casey asked.

Douglas took a sip of his coffee. "I dunno. I have all those boxes in the storage locker and to tell you the truth I have no idea what's in any of them. Maybe if we catch a few days off sometime you can help me look through."

"Whenever you want. Sounds like fun."

"Yeah, sorry," McAfee snorted. "I'm busy that day."

They laughed and Casey encouraged Douglas to continue. "Okay, I know it sucks, but let's hear the bad."

Douglas nodded and took one more sip of coffee. "Okay. Well, let me say this first. I'm following your guidelines and talking about things from before we met. Because the truth is that seeing you in prison for Christmas was horrible. It broke my heart. But it wasn't the first time. You guys both know that. It's not even real easy to decide which was the worst because God knows lots of them were hard. When my ex took my daughter from me years ago that first Christmas boy...that was rough. She wouldn't let me speak to her, much less see her. And by that point she'd poisoned her against me so badly that it wouldn't have mattered much anyway. But beside that, the hardest Christmas was the first one that Mama and I spent alone.

My Daddy had just died. My brother's overdose and my sister's murder had been years earlier. It was dark in ways that I'd never experienced before. Mama wasn't doing well and I knew it. She was ashy and frail. She seemed confused over the tiniest of things. I'd try to engage with her but she just wasn't following. Nothing big, you know, local gossip on businesses coming and going and who had grandchildren on the way. She'd just nod a bit, not making much eye contact, kinda looking off into...I don't know, the past maybe."

Casey took hold of his hand and gave it a little squeeze.

"So," he continued, "Christmas eve came and I did my best to make that ham and those sweet rolls. I couldn't cook like Mama of course but I did my best. I went and got a small tree, just one of those table top ones but a real one, you know. I put the lights on and knelt down beside Mama in her chair. I took hold of her hand and said the prayer for what was left of our family. Just her and me. I had no more Dad, no more siblings, no wife or daughter. But I wanted to try and give Mama a nice Christmas. Just like all the ones she'd given to us. When I said the prayer though she just kinda sighed. She touched my cheek for just a moment and said, "It's no use baby." Then she got up, went into her bedroom, and closed the door. So, yeah, that one was really hard."

McAfee shook his head and looked at Casey. "This is bullshit, Malone. It's Christmas for...I mean, what the hell?"

"It's healing. That's what Christmas is about Mac."

"I thought it was about the birth of Jesus and goodwill on earth and all of that."

"Yup. And what was the point of Jesus coming to earth?"

"Oh for fuck's sake," he turned to Douglas. "What the hell?"

"Just do it old man," Casey ordered him. "Knock off your whiny shit and do it!"

"Fine Malone! You pain in the goddamn ass!"

Casey smiled sweetly. "Thank you. You may proceed. We're all ears."

Douglas hid his smile behind his coffee cup as Mac shot him one final look. Then he clearly accepted that he was going to do exactly as Casey wanted and relaxed his shoulders as he sat back in his chair. "Well," he took a sip of his coffee. The best one first, right?"

"Whichever you'd like," Casey answered softly.

"Alright, whatever. Here goes...

There was a youth outreach officer that would often visit Lloyd's High school and spend some time talking with some of the kids about possible careers in law enforcement and the steps they should be taking now if they thought they might want to pursue one of those opportunities. It wasn't ever super formal, just some conversations outside on the basketball court or maybe in the cafeteria. But if you decided you wanted to really reach for that as a goal then you'd be invited to join the explorer program. It was similar in many ways to the military track ROTC program, but developed to help young people maneuver toward education and training goals that would help them eventually secure jobs in law enforcement. They'd work with the youth services officer in a classroom setting, learning about everything from the Constitution to racial diversity. They'd engage in physical activities as well, from running to weight training to self defense classes. It was all intended to give you a head start when the time came to join the academy. Or, if you were headed off to college, to at least know how to maintain your physical fitness while you were there.

The young McAfee had something that his fellow explorers didn't have, legacy status. His Dad was a drunk. He was a shitbag, abusive, mean, drunk. But, he was also a very respected homicide detective with the highest closure rate in his division. He worked long and unpredictable hours, often staying away for days at a time. Lloyd didn't know it as a young boy but later on he realized his Dad was most likely sitting in a bar a lot of the times when his Mama thought he was working. The one thing he was pretty sure of was that his Dad didn't give a crap about him. All his father wanted when he got home was for him and his brothers to stay quiet in their rooms while their poor mother served him the best food she could muster, often just to have it thrown in her face.

Lloyd tried all the time to do things that would make his father proud of him, thinking maybe if he did then his father would be less mean to his Mom and maybe even spend some time with him. He wanted to ask him so many questions. What was it like to be a cop? What was the hardest case he ever worked? Did he ever have to pull his weapon? Was he scared? But most days he was too afraid to even say hello to his old man, much less try to strike up a conversation. The guy just had no use for him, it was obvious. So what could you do? The youth officer answered the questions that he wanted to ask his Dad and he'd just have to make do with that.

It was just before Christmas break of his senior year. There was only six months left to go before he'd graduate and be eligible to apply to the academy. You got to graduate from the explorer program at that point so that you could spend the last six months of your high school career serving as a mentor to the younger kids who wanted to join the explorers. There was a ceremony in the gym that all the kids came to see, and you were welcome to invite your parents to come as well. Lloyd's mother had been beaming that morning, straightening his tie and telling him how very proud she was. She was going to be at the school nice and early, she promised, so that she could get a good seat right up front on the bleachers. When the time came to receive your completion badge then your parents were invited to come up and be the ones to pin it on you.

Like all school assemblies it was packed and loud. Kids were shouting to one another and family members were making their way in to find seats. But despite the chaos he spotted her, sitting there in her best dress with a huge smile on her face. She waved enthusiastically at him and he knew in his heart that this moment was making his mother feel proud. He waved one more time before turning away, afraid that the other kids would see him getting emotional. When the ceremony began the eleven graduating explorers lined up to be called one by one to the stage in alphabetical order. Each student would be called by name and then their parents would be introduced to come and pin on their tiny badge. The youth officer who ran the program called them one by one and would pause so photos could be taken by a police department photographer. And then it was Lloyd's turn. His name was called and he walked up to stand at attention and wait for his Mama to come pin on his badge. The officer spoke into the microphone. "Please welcome Officer McAfee's mother, Mrs. Anna McAfee. And it is my great pleasure to also welcome a hero of the Atlanta police department, Veteran Detective Jonathan McAfee.

He felt his face go flush. His eyes shifted ever so slightly where he stood at attention to see his Mother and Father approach the podium, arm in arm, and shake hands with the youth officer. They made their way over to him and he saw his mother wipe away a tear. But it was his Dad who pinned on the badge, looking him straight in the eye and winking before taking him in his arms and whispering into his ear. "I'm proud of you boy." He was damn near in shock as his father took two steps back before formally saluting his son and then...smiling.

Mac stopped talking and went back to sipping his coffee. Douglas and Casey stayed quiet for a few moments and waited for him to say something. He finally turned to them. "Yeah, so, that was pretty cool. Not really a Christmas story but that's what I remember most from that year. There were decorations hanging in the gym and they were getting ready for the Christmas ball. But my old man even showing up, much less hugging me. Course, he did that at my academy graduation also but he got his ass kissed at that one by pretty much everybody and didn't spend much time on me. But he did pin my shield on. So, yeah."

Casey smiled. "Thank you for telling us that."

"Yeah, you're welcome Malone."

"See, we're bonding."

McAfee grinned. "I had a lot of great Christmas's after that with my own kids of course but that one just popped in my head."

"His approval was important to you," Douglas offered.

"I guess so. Fathers and sons, right."

"So, the worst?" Casey asked.

Mac crossed his legs and looked at her a moment. "You sure you really wanna hear this stuff Malone? You've been through some pretty heavy stuff already without making things even darker."

"I think that airing it out helps to heal it. And since I feel so close to you guys I want to do this with you."

He shrugged, took a breath, and began…

Nobody wanted to catch the night shift, especially on Christmas eve. But the rotation was set in the beginning of the year. You got to choose what days you wanted and if some other detective who had seniority picked the same day then tough luck for you. McAfee had had twelve years on the job at that point, four with his gold shield. He'd done his first two working mostly vice cases in the seediest parts of the city before getting noticed by one of the hot shot homicide detectives and getting bumped up to major crimes. His division handled homicide but usually the more senior guys caught those cases. Mac was mostly working sexual assault and armed robbery cases, sometimes being assigned to a team on a murder case to do some grunt footwork and interviews. But rotation meant you handled your regular caseload plus whatever might pop up on the night you were covering.

It was freezing. People didn't realize that Atlanta got that cold but they'd see about three inches of snow each year. Though not all at once. It was busy, as you'd expect Christmas eve to be. He'd parked his car on the street in front of a small jewelry store in the shopping district and just sat. He'd learned from his years on the job that if a cop just sat and watched, sooner or later something was gonna go down. It was just before ten, the stores were serving their final holiday customers and getting ready to shut down. He'd leaned back in his seat and rested, eyes slowly searching back and forth for any sign of trouble. What kind of trouble? Who knew? Maybe an armed robbery. These retail stores were raking it in big today serving all the happy people hyped up on Christmas spirit and blowing their savings. Young women in their tight sparkly skirts were walking in and out of bars by themselves. Young couples were strolling hand in hand past dark alleys, their attention on the beautiful Christmas lights and not on the possible dangers around them.

He knew it of course. He thought like a cop. Most people can go out for a pleasant evening and enjoy themselves without thinking about all the horrible ways they might become a victim. But there were far too many for whom that trust was violated. People who had gone to dinner, or the store, or for a jog, or for a blind date, and who would never be the same again. McAfee wasn't sitting in his car watching all the fun that people were having. He was searching for thieves, for con artists, for pickpockets, and most of all, for predators. He knew instinctively who belonged in that particular environment and who stuck out somehow. He could see it in their eyes, read it in the expressions. He could see them watching for an opportunity, just as he was watching for someone to take advantage of such an opportunity.

It was about five minutes till ten when he spotted her. She stuck out like a sore thumb as she came out of an alley where a girl that young had no reason to be. He was about half a block down but he moved quickly, catching up with her and keeping pace as she walked along the sidewalk, dodging shoppers and carolers and headed very determinedly for someplace. He guessed that she was maybe fifteen, give or take a year. She was dressed well, clean. Definitely not a street kid. Somebody was taking care of her. But she was a minor, on the street alone after normal business hours. He was justified to question her.

"Miss?" he called out.

She kept moving.

"Miss? Young lady? Hold up."

She turned to see if someone was in fact calling out to her and when she spotted McAfee she quickened her pace.

"Miss!, Come on now. Police."

She turned once more and he held up his badge. She stopped and waited for him to catch up.

"Hey there. Boy, you move quick. Where you heading to sweetheart?"

She looked nervous but lots of people react to the police that way. Most folks go their entire lives without any interaction with a cop. Plus she was young, maybe younger than he'd thought.

"Just home," she answered quietly, looking down at her shoes.

"Oh okay, that's good. It's getting a bit late now."

She nodded.

"What's your name love?"

"Marcy," she answered.

"Hi Marcy, I'm Lloyd. What's your last name?"

He saw her hesitate for a moment before answering. "Jones."

She made eye contact for a moment and he smiled. "That's a great name kid. But it's not yours now is it?"

Her eyes went back to her shoes and she shook her head no.

"Okay. It's okay. Lots of people are wary of the cops. I get it. You're not in trouble okay? I'm just checking on you. So what's your real name?"

The girl sighed. "Marcy. Marcy Benton."

"Marcy Benton? That so?"

She nodded yes and he knew she was telling the truth.

"How old are you, Miss Marcy?"

"Fourteen."

"Oh okay, great. Eighth grade?"

"Ninth."

"Oh, high school."

"Yes sir."

"So, you must live close by since you're walking?"

She hesitated once more but quickly seemed resigned to her circumstance.

"Magnolia terrace."

"Oh okay. Nice building. That's a good eight blocks up still."

"Yes sir."

"Well, no trouble. Like I said, I just wanna see you get home okay."

He hadn't expected her to take off running but she did. He was in decent shape back then, but not high school shape. It didn't matter though because she wasn't moving quite as fast as she should have been. In fact, she seemed to possibly be hurt. He caught up easily to the girl who was now sobbing and bending over. It was then that he noticed the blood on the front of her jeans. He opened his arms and she allowed him to hold her as she cried. He was already planning through the process in his head for dealing with a rape victim. She was shivering and he removed his sport jacket to wrap around her, slowly walking her back toward his car. When they had reached it he got her safely belted into the passenger seat and cranked up the heat. He climbed in behind the wheel and waited silently for a few moments.

"I'm on your side. Okay?"

She looked away from him, watching the sidewalk fill up as the last of the stores began to empty out.

"No matter what?" she asked and wiped her nose with her sleeve.

He reached into the glove box and grabbed a pack of tissues. "No matter what. You can tell me."

She was reluctant at first and he didn't push. Every victim was different and they each reacted and interacted in their own way. She didn't say it, which was also not unusual. She simply said, "In the alley."

He pulled his car out and drove up to the dark alley, turning in but moving very slowly in case her attacker or attackers might still be there. He turned on his high beams but didn't see any movement at all. She pointed forward and he drove another thirty feet or so.

"There," she pointed.

He looked out of her window and followed her finger.

"The dumpster?"

She nodded.

He climbed out and approached the dumpster slowly. Normally his hand would be on his weapon but he knew already that would not be necessary. There was nobody else in the alley and nobody else had been. Just her. Just frightened little fourteen year old Marcy Benton. He lifted the lid and aimed his flashlight inside. He spotted it immediately, pulled back the material just to be sure. He suddenly felt much colder, chilled to the bone. He exhaled and reached in to check but he already knew. He walked back around the car and climbed back in beside the sobbing child in his front seat. He put his arm around her and hugged her tightly, telling her softly that everything would be okay. He grabbed his radio mic and pushed the button. "Seven-eight."

"Go ahead seven-eight," a dispatcher answered.

"One eighty seven at my location. Infant child."

Casey felt her eyes moisten as McAfee told his story. When he stopped it was if she'd just been a witness to it herself.

"Was the baby already…?"

He shook his head. "She hadn't even known she was pregnant till about eight weeks before and even then she wasn't certain. She'd been terrified about her parents finding out and so when she felt the baby coming she'd made her way down toward the shopping district, thinking at first that she'd give birth in a bathroom and just leave the baby there for someone to find. But when the baby started to come she found her way into that alley. She said she just held her hand over his face, just trying to keep him quiet so she wouldn't get in any trouble."

"Dear God," Douglas shook his head.

"Yeah, so, worst Christmas. Seeing that tiny baby in a dumpster."

It was nearly nine a.m. The sun was coming up brighter behind the building opposite them and it had begun to warm up a bit more. Not that it had been cold. The days had been a pleasant sixty to sixty-five degrees in Atlanta that week, not at all like the Christmas eve weather that

Mac had just described. Casey curled her legs up beneath her on the swing. "Okay, my turn."

"You really don't have to do this," Douglas told her. "Mac's right. This is a bit heavy for Christmas."

"No," she smiled. "I want to. Don't you guys see that this is stuff we should all know about each other. A family should know this stuff."

Douglas and Mac exchanged a quick glance, fully understanding Casey's desire to be able to share like this when she'd never had that in her life before.

"Okay, my best Christmas before you guys…"

Her Mama had let her go to Emma's since there wasn't nuthin going on at their house for the holiday. Casey had never experienced Christmas, a birthday party, or none of that her entire life until Emma had come along. Her family seemed to celebrate everything. You got a good grade? Then that called for a special dinner. A new client at work? A special dinner. Every holiday there was a barbecue or a party or at least a small family celebration. Their lives were so completely different from her own that it seemed like she was transported into one of those family tv shows whenever she was with them. It just never seemed real to her. But real or not, she loved being at their house.

When she had been younger, a kindly bookstore owner had given her the only Christmas gift she had ever received. It might not have seemed like all that much to some folks, but she had wanted to read the book he'd given her so badly and when he told her it was hers it was pure joy. She'd been so excited to get home and read it. But her Mama had been mad on account of her getting home a little late for dinner, not that she'd cooked or anything, and also cause she'd slipped on her bike and got her clothes muddy. So she'd taken the book away, forbidden her to see the "pervert who owns that place," again, and that was that.

She was in High School now, and had become close friends with Emma and Sasha. Those friendships had made her life bearable. There were still some very dark days, painful days, but at least now she had people who cared about her that she could talk to. She'd tell them all the time don't y'all be worryin' on me so much. But they did. They worried because they cared. They told her they loved her because they did. And she knew it.

Her Mama had been heading out to drink with her friends and she knew at that point that Casey shouldn't be at home alone with her Daddy. So she'd given her permission to go spend the day with Emma's family as long as she got her ass back in the house by nine and didn't talk none about their family business while she was over there. So she'd worn the best dress she had and ridden her bike to their place, feeling awkward that she didn't have anything to bring for their table or a small gift maybe. They didn't care though. Everybody had hugged her and made her feel so welcome that she forgot about her own life for a few hours. The food was amazing, unlike anything she'd ever experienced, but the sounds...of joking and laughter, even singing. It made her feel as if she was smiling on the inside.

The best part had come after dinner, when Emma's Mama had called for them all to sit in the living room, cheerfully announcing that it was time to open presents. Casey had sat on the far end of the sofa so that she wouldn't be in the way of their family time. But Emma took her hand and excitedly pulled her closer to her and the stack of presents beneath the tree. Then it happened, her Mama began to pass out the gifts. "Carl, Emma, Riley, Casey." At first she was stunned. She thought that she must have heard her wrong. But she didn't. Emma passed the gift to her and she sat there completely surprised as the others began to tear open the paper. Emma's Mom had come and sat down beside Casey and gently rubbed her hand. "Open your present, Casey."

Casey became aware that they were all looking at her now and she answered shyly. "You got a present for me?"

Emma's Mom put her arm around her and hugged her tight. "Of course we did. You're part of the family."

They were all smiling at her now, not mocking, not like at home. These were genuine smiles. She opened the package slowly, being ever so careful not to tear the beautiful wrapping paper. When she saw it she couldn't hold back the tears.

"What is it Casey?" Emma asked happily. "Show us."

Casey held it up for them to see. "It's a copy of the book that my Mama threw away."

Casey smiled as she repeated the happy memory. "I was so happy that day. That wasn't the only gift either. They got me a nice outfit for school and a beautiful diary with a lock and everything ."

"They are an incredible family," Douglas smiled. "You are really fortunate to have them in your life."

"I know it. They told me that I would always be a part of their family and that I was welcome to be there with them any time I chose for the rest of my life."

"Wow," McAfee said.

"Yeah, I know."

"Emma and Sasha are both great girls," Douglas added. "I'm looking forward to seeing them later."

"Me too. So, the bad. I won't drag it out. There's no long story to it. My worst Christmas was the same day as my best."

"Oh no," Mac answered.

"Yes. I asked Emma if I could keep my gifts there so that nobody took them away or messed with them. She said she was going to empty a drawer in her dresser and that was gonna be my drawer from then on. I gave them all a hug and headed home at eight thirty. Like I said, no long story. You both already know it. My Mama wasn't home when I got there but Daddy was. You know what happened."

Douglas pulled her to him and hugged her tightly. After a moment Casey checked her watch. "Okay, time to get ready for the mall."

She turned to McAfee. "Come on old man."

It was just after noon when they returned. Douglas had just basted the turkey for the third time and the wonderful aroma of the meal to come filled the condo. Casey was excited to see that the tree had been delivered as well and Douglas had already pulled the bins out of the hallway storage closet with the ornaments and lights.

"Looks like you've been busy."

"Y'all too. How many bags do you have there?"

"Too many," Mac answered. "The girl can shop. And quick."

"Found everything you were looking for?"

"Yes," she answered. "And I see you've been doing some wrapping as well."

"I may have hit a couple shops in Savannah and did some online ordering," he grinned. "Mac and I had a little time to browse while you and Dede were at the beach."

"I wanna call her later and check on them."

"Good idea. I'm sure she'll be happy to hear from you."

They spent the afternoon decorating the tree, wrapping gifts and prepping the rest of the food for dinner. By five-thirty it was dark, the tree was lit along with some candles on the table, and soft Christmas classics were playing on the turntable. They sat down to the first restful meal that they'd had in weeks and enjoyed every moment of it. By the time they got back up from the table they were all thoroughly stuffed. They were expecting Emma and Sasha as well as Sammy and her boyfriend to stop by for coffee and dessert so they cleared the table and retired to the living room to open gifts while they waited. Douglas had found her a beautiful bracelet in Savannah and had been clearly paying attention when she'd pointed out clothes she liked in magazine ads because he nailed it with all of them. Casey had found Douglas a shirt and tie set that he loved as well as a world's best dad mug that choked him up a bit. McAfee even seemed to get a bit emotional when he opened his world's best uncle mug but he quickly recovered and mumbled, "Thanks kid."

The others had all arrived by seven and the place livened up a bit. The music turned more jovial and everyone enjoyed the pie and Christmas cookies. Casey and her friends went into her room to call Dede and wish her a merry Christmas while the others sipped their coffee.

"Your story is front- page this Sunday," Sammy said. "Since it's a holiday weekend the readership should be bigger than our usual Sunday run."

Douglas put his hand on her shoulder. "Thank you again for everything you did to help. With the story and with getting them settled."

"Of course Douglas. You guys did amazing work on this one."

"We're not done yet," McAfee assured her as he joined them.

"Just be careful you guys. These are powerful people."

"I'm just really glad we made it back home for Christmas," Douglas said. "It was really important that we be here."

"I understand. She looks really happy Douglas. And...adjusted."

He nodded. "I think she's healing more and more each day."

Casey, Emma and Sasha joined them all back in the living room and sang along a bit to the music.

"How is she?" Douglas asked.

"They sound really happy," Casey answered. "Which makes me happy."

"So girls," Sammy smiled. "You ladies gonna hit the clubs for New Year's?"

"Nope," Casey answered. "I'm gonna hit the books and try to get back in the groove before school starts back. Plus, Douglas got me two new novels and I'm fixin' to relax and read them both."

"What she means is, yes, we're going to the club for new year's," Sasha rolled her eyes.

"No, no you guys," Casey objected. "We already talked about this."

"You mean you talked about it," Emma poked her. "We're going out though. Little skirts, a whole lotta flirting with the boys…"

Casey laughed. "Stop it. I'm staying right here at home. Tell them Douglas."

"I think a fun night out with your friends is just what you need," he smiled.

"See!" Sasha pointed at her. "You are not staying home and geeking out on us."

"We'll see."

"Girl please. You know we're gonna have our way with you. Just accept it."

Everyone had enjoyed themselves so much that it was nearly midnight before the party broke up. Mac headed back to his place and the others headed off to get some rest before their family get- togethers on Christmas morning. Casey and Douglas grabbed what was left of the pie and headed out to their new swing.

"So, this one was definitely a great Christmas," Douglas smiled as she cuddled up beside him.

"It was awesome. And we have tons of food for tomorrow just for us. So much for getting back on my diet when we got home."

"That's what New year's resolutions are for."

"So I get to welcome in the new year in my fat pants."

"I can't believe we were gone so long. It felt so good to be in my own shower."

"Oh gosh I know. I missed my bed."

"This one was hard all around."

"Yeah, it was."

"Just make sure that if you ever feel like you don't wanna do this you let me know."

"Do what? Eat pie? That won't ever happen."

Douglas laughed.

"I know," she smiled. "But just think if we hadn't done this one."

"Yeah," he agreed.

"I keep thinking about how many people are out there like Jeremy and Dede...and me."

"Sammy just told me earlier that people are actually starting to request us on a regular basis. They have stories to tell and want us to be the ones to help them do it."

"That makes me happy."

"Yeah, me too."

"But let's wait till after New Year's. I have new books to read."

Douglas laughed. "Okay kid. After New year's it is."

Week Five

Bella sat in the bus station and waited. Just like she did on most nights. There was more traffic than usual as people returned from their holiday trips around the country. It was now January second, a whole new year had arrived and everybody seemed so excited. For her it was the same old. New year's eve had been pretty busy with the college boys home from school. They had barely settled into the new place before it was party central. That bitch Dede had really messed things up for the rest of them. Not only did they have their regular work to do but they had been on moving and unpacking duty as well. On top of that the new place was not nearly as nice as the downtown apartment had been. Somehow it had all ended up being her fault since she was the one who had "recruited" Dede.

She was the best at what she did. That's what they always told her. Not that what she did was anything she could be proud of. It did however keep her from being beaten or pimped out at a street level or even killed. Her ability to do what she did was saving her right now. She needed to make up for the whole fiasco with Dede. They had lost a fortune on that one. A couple of the bosses had gone down including the one that paid off the cops and handled the judges. They had been infuriated to the point that she feared for her life. Maybe they wouldn't like the idea of a link to themselves by way of her. But after a couple of weeks they'd determined that it was over. Conrad Nash had been the target and now they had all moved on and it could go back to business as usual. It was just politics they said. Powerful people wanted Nash gone and now he was. And so now here she was.

Her talent was reading people. She could instantly spot who was out of place, who was scared or worried or emotional. She could see who had a clear direction and who did not. Some people came off the buses with a quick step, headed home or to family or work. Others came off looking sorry that the ride had come to an end because the end represented nothing to them. At best things would be a challenge for them and at worst an absolute threat. Some people came off the bus with life experiences that they could use, intuition they could rely on. Others arrived from small towns and remote areas where life was far different than life in the big scary city. Bella had a talent for reading all of them, spotting that one gem that would make her bosses happy and earn them money. Maybe it was nothing to be proud of, but it helped her survive.

They were shuffling past her now in throngs, pulling their rolling suitcases behind them or hoisting on their backpacks. Some of them headed quickly into the bathrooms as if they expected to explode at any moment. Others hugged waiting family members or friends or headed over to the waiting taxis and Ubers. She wasn't looking for any of them. Bella was searching for that one girl who looked lost. That one young girl who came off the bus looking haunted and completely alone. A girl who seemed both terrified and relieved at the same time. Somebody who had made the decision to risk the unknown darkness in order to escape the one she knew too well. And right there, coming off of the number sixteen, was just such a girl.

She was damn near cowering, averting her eyes and clearly trying to stay off the radar of the patrol cop talking to the pretty magazine peddler just across the way. She was country for sure. Bella could see it in her clothes and in the very way that she walked. She was cute. Kinda a pretty little thing actually and that was without makeup or a decent outfit. There was no doubt that the guys would like her. More importantly they'd be willing to pay for her. She looked uncertain of which way to go, carrying her worn out backpack toward one of the benches and plopping herself down to wait for the world to give her a sign. Maybe send her a savior. It was time to pounce.

Bella made her way over and casually sat down beside the girl.

"Oh sorry, do you mind?"

The girl shook her head no, still avoiding eye contact.

"This place is so crowded tonight. I just got back from visiting my parents but my friends aren't here yet to pick me up."

The girl nodded.

"So, yeah, I can't wait to get home and get some food. My roomies said they cooked a lasagna and some fresh bread and my mouth is watering just thinking about it."

"That sounds nice," the girl answered.

"How about you? You waiting on someone?"

The girl shrugged.

"I know how it is. I pretty much keep to myself too. Until I met these girls I didn't know anybody here either. I came into town, met one of them, had a place to stay and a job within three days."

The girl turned to her now. "For real?"

"Yeah I was so relieved. But now we're stressing cause one of them moved out and we need a fourth to help pay the rent. Hey, you wouldn't be interested in coming in with us, would you?"

"I don't have any money."

"Oh, no worries. We could float you till you find something. I guarantee we can get you going within a couple days. God knows we have more than enough food to share."

"I dunno," she looked away again.

"Yeah I get it. It's cool. Well, nice talking to you anyway. Good luck in the city. Just be careful girl. It can be really dangerous out there."

Bella got up and began to walk away toward the entrance. She grinned when she heard the girl call out, "Hey, wait!"

She walked back as the girl stood up to face her. She was actually really pretty, wholesome looking. Guys liked blondes that was for sure. A little mini skirt and the right top…

"You change your mind?"

"You sure it's okay that I don't have any cash?"

"Girl, you're gonna be working faster than you think."

"Don't you need to check with your roommates or something first?"

"Believe me they will be thrilled. They won't want their own bills going up," she laughed.

"If you're really sure."

"You gotta be as hungry as me. Come on home with me and eat and meet the other girls. If it's not for you, no hard feelings."

The girl nodded, looking relieved. "Okay, thank you, uh…"

"Bella. My name's Bella."

"I'm really glad I met up with you Bella. My name's Casey."

"And my name's Lloyd McAfee," came a voice from behind her. Bella turned to look at the large man and instinctively knew he was a cop. After all, she knew how to read people so well.

www.ingramcontent.com/pod-product-compliance
Lightning Source LLC
La Vergne TN
LVHW050620100826
845148LV00011B/1662